KRISTY FOR PRESIDENT

Other books by
Ann M. Martin

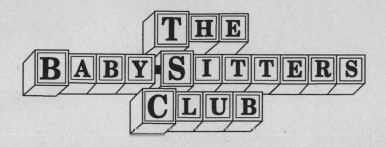

KRISTY FOR PRESIDENT

Ann M. Martin

AN
APPLE
PAPERBACK

SCHOLASTIC INC.
New York Toronto London Auckland Sydney

Cover art by Hodges Soileau

No part of this publication may be reproduced in whole or in part, or stored in a retrieval system, or transmitted in any form or by any means, electronic, mechanical, photocopying, recording, or otherwise, without written permission of the publisher. For information regarding permission, write to Scholastic Inc., 555 Broadway, New York, NY 10012.

ISBN 0-590-92578-4

12 11 10 9 8 7 6 5 4 3 2   10   7 8 9/9 0 1/0

Printed in the U.S.A.   40

The author gratefully acknowledges
Nola Thacker
for her help in
preparing this manuscript.

KRISTY FOR PRESIDENT

CHAPTER 1

Friday. Finally. And was I ever glad. It's too bad you can't organize the weeks so that Fridays come more often. Or so that you have extra ones to use every once in awhile, when you need them — like those cards in Monopoly to Get Out of Jail Free. Not that I think of Stoneybrook Middle School as jail.

But if Friday had just come earlier this week, I would have missed a pop quiz in science on Wednesday, for example. I didn't fail it. But I wasn't ready for ten true-false questions about the similarities and differences between vertebrates and invertebrates.

At least it was Friday now. The PA system was just finishing crackling and garbling out announcements, which sounded like someone with his hand over his mouth practicing ventriloquism. (Stacey McGill says it brings a little bit of New York City here to Stoneybrook,

Connecticut, because that's how all the announcements in the subways sound.) After the announcements we'd be going to an assembly.

Stacey is from New York originally. She's a little more sophisticated than the rest of us. The rest of us isn't all of Stoneybrook Middle School, although she often *does* seem older than everyone else at SMS. The "us" I'm talking about is the Baby-sitters Club. That's a business that my six friends and I operate. I'm the president and Stacey is the treasurer and — well — more about that later.

When the announcements were over, and the bell had rung, I picked up my books and headed for the auditorium. Stacey and Claudia Kishi were going in just as I got there. Stacey and Claudia are best friends — they share a sort of city-cool sense of style, for one thing — and Claud is also vice-president of the BSC.

"Friday at last," said Claudia, as if she'd been reading my mind. Claudia is not too fond of school. In fact, you could probably say school is not her best subject, although she is smart and very creative.

"Does anybody know what this assembly is about?" I asked.

"Maybe," Claudia said, "they're going to cancel school for the rest of the day."

"Good idea," I replied.

2

"In your dreams," said Stacey, shaking her head. Claudia and I grinned at each other and followed Stacey into the auditorium.

Mary Anne Spier and Dawn Schafer were saving us seats.

I plopped down next to Mary Anne. "Whew! This week has been too long."

Mary Anne looked at me sympathetically. She knew about that pop quiz. "I couldn't do everything you do, Kristy," she said. "It's amazing."

I thought about that and felt better: baby-sitting, coaching the Krushers, which is what you might call a well-rounded softball team (the youngest player is only two and a half and the oldest is eight), being president of the Baby-sitters Club, and keeping up with school *is* a pretty tough schedule. I raised my eyebrows and said, in a snobby tone, *"Organization. If one is organized, one can do anything."*

Mary Anne made a face, then suddenly lifted her arm and waved. Mallory Pike and Jessi Ramsey, who are sixth-graders and junior officers in the BSC, hurried to join us. Jessi was giggling and Mal was rolling her eyes, but before we could talk anymore, the assembly was called to order.

It was *not* the most interesting assembly in the history of the school. In fact, it was more like having the PA announcements read clearly and in person. About five minutes after it started I looked down the row of seats and saw:

Stacey, staring into space, fiddling with one of her earrings (a small silver replica of the Eiffel Tower). Claudia, her head bent, her long black hair, which was swept up and over to one side, falling forward over her cheek as she drew something in her notebook. Dawn, doing some quick catch-up homework. Mal, just plain reading — probably a horse story. Jessi, sitting very upright, one leg raised, flexing her ankle. Mary Anne, not doing anything quite so obvious to show she was bored, but glancing around — very casually, of course. Probably looking for Logan Bruno, who is her boyfriend.

I snuck a quick look around myself, wishing Bart Taylor went to our school. I sort of have a crush on Bart. Okay — I have a giant crush on him. Then I noticed the Special Ed kids. Like the BSC, they were all sitting together. But then they do everything together, even staying in the same classroom although the other students change classes.

Sometimes the other students — the "normal" ones — make fun of the Special Ed kids.

4

I couldn't help wondering whether if we saw more of them, it would happen less. I mean, I know the world is not perfect, and you can't change everybody. But you have to try, right?

What would I do, I wondered, remembering Susan, a girl who is autistic. I'd baby-sat for her not too long ago. That job — and Susan — had taught me to look at the Special Ed kids almost as if I were seeing them for the first time, which in a way I guess I was. "Learning different." That was a phrase I'd heard used. They learned different things differently — the way Stacey was a whiz in math and Claudia saw the world full of possibilities for creating new sculptures and drawings and paintings.

Susan was locked up in her own world, as if the world outside didn't exist at all. She was away now at a school that probably had the best possible chance of helping her. But these kids were right here. What if —

"Kristy?"

Mary Anne was poking me, and I figured the assembly was over.

Then I realized it wasn't over at all. It was a fire drill.

"Just in time," said Stacey. She nodded toward the stage, where the principal was thumping on the microphone, making it give out one of those EEEEE-NNNNNNN sounds, like fingernails on the chalkboard with the volume way up.

Mary Anne clapped her hands over her ears and made a face, and we all stood up obediently.

The principal was saying something, but you couldn't understand it. Fortunately, there had been so many fire drills lately that we were pretty experienced at handling them. There was a lot of shuffling and giggling and teachers clapping and making motions like traffic cops. I heard a shriek and whipped around. Maybe the school really was on fire. But then I saw Cokie Mason, her face red. She was rubbing her shoulder and glaring at Alan Gray. He'd obviously just given her one of his dumb knuckle punches.

Alan Gray is such a goon sometimes.

"I bet that hurt," said Mary Anne, *almost* sympathetically. That's Mary Anne. She can be sympathetic to the most rotten people. And considering some of the tricks Cokie Mason has pulled on Mary Anne (and on me, for that matter), Cokie should be at the top of Mary Anne's rotten-people list.

Thinking about that, I decided maybe, just this once, Alan wasn't being such a goon. "Probably another false alarm," I said.

"Yeah," said Claudia. "I like missing class, but this is a little *extreme*."

Everyone got outside pretty quickly. Since we had all been in the same place this was easier than usual. I noticed that some of the kids seemed to be drifting away, toward the sidewalk. I looked back at the school, half expecting to see smoke pouring out and teachers motioning us farther away to safety. But SMS just stood there stolidly, the same as always.

I looked back and more kids were following. I couldn't believe it. Then one of the substitute teachers, Mr. Zorzi, walked quickly by. A minute later we saw him at the head of the group of kids, his arms held up.

The mass exit from the school grounds stopped.

Claud started to laugh. "I don't believe it," she said. "Alan and the other guys just started walking and everyone followed."

She was right. Another teacher had gone out to join Mr. Zorzi and they came back, leading Alan Gray and Justin Forbes and Kelsey Bauman. Alan and his friends looked sort of sheepish, but you could tell by the way they were glancing sideways at people and grinning a little that they were pleased with themselves, too.

Stacey shook her head. "Would you follow those guys anywhere?"

"No way," said Dawn.

"Not a trusty leader," agreed Claudia.

After an assembly (well, half an assembly) and a fire alarm, the rest of the morning went by pretty quickly. And despite all the variations in our morning routine, what was being served up for lunch looked just the same.

"What *is* that stuff?" I asked Claudia.

Claudia peered down at her plate. "I like to think of it as art," she said loftily.

"Splatter art," I agreed. "You know, like in those horror movies . . ."

"Ewww. Kristy!"

"Don't worry, Stacey," I said soothingly. "You didn't get the hot lunch."

Dawn, who was placidly opening a container of yogurt to go with her sprout salad, said, "I believe that is called meat loaf."

Mary Anne picked up her fork and started to cut the meat loaf. Just as she cut it, I shrieked.

Mary Anne gave a little shriek herself and dropped the fork. I lowered my voice mysteriously. "I think it's still alive."

Everyone broke up, except Mary Anne, who was looking a little green. She gave me a Look, and I said, "Okay, okay."

I picked up my own fork and took another look at the meat loaf. It was gray, and the tomato sauce was pale red and watery. The mashed potatoes next to it had a sort of oozy quality. And I wasn't so sure I liked the color of the broccoli. It looked like something that had been attacked by Bunnicula, the vampire rabbit.

I sniffed at my lunch. "This does not smell great," I said.

"No," said Dawn, who is totally into healthy food.

"I can't believe they keep serving us stuff like this. It can't be good for you."

"No," repeated Dawn.

"You know, Kristy," said Stacey, who also brings her own lunch, "why don't you do something about it? Class president elections are coming up. Run for class president."

"Maybe." I gave the broccoli a poke, decided it was safe even if Bunnicula had gotten there first, and started to eat. I had forgotten it was almost time for class elections. It was probably one of the things that was going to be talked about in the assembly. The requirements were not any big deal. The main one was that you had to have a B average.

That part, at least, would be no sweat.

"You could," said Stacey, polishing off the

apple she'd brought for dessert. She pointed to the soggy piece of angel food cake on my tray, which was beginning to look a little too much like the mashed potatoes. "Your motto could be 'Let us eat cake.' "

Everyone cracked up.

CHAPTER 2

If Friday was wild and crazy, Saturday was pretty usual — wild and crazy.

Nannie and I ate breakfast to the sound of live music. Nannie is my — our — grandmother. Not too long ago, Mom got married again. (Our dad left when I was a little kid. He lives in California, and we never really hear from him.) Mom married Watson Brewer, and we had to move into Watson's house. Okay, it's actually a mansion, and moving wasn't so bad, although I hated to leave because I lived right next door to Mary Anne and across the street from Claudia.

But life in a mansion is okay. Before this, Sam and Charlie, my two older brothers who are at Stoneybrook High School, had to share a room. And David Michael, who is a second-grader, practically lived in a closet. Now we all have our own rooms. But we're filling the mansion up pretty fast. Watson's two kids,

11

Karen, who is seven like David Michael, and Andrew, who is almost five, spend every other weekend with us and two weeks during the summer. And then there's Emily Michelle. She's our adopted sister. She's from Vietnam and is two and a half.

And that's where Nannie comes in. Watson and Mom both work hard, and so Mom asked her mother to come live with us and help while everyone is at work or at school. And she did.

So that's Nannie.

Breakfast was English muffins, toasted, with peanut butter and strawberry jam for me and plum preserves for Nannie.

The music was Karen and David Michael singing in the den. They'd made up this game to the tune of "Do-Re-Mi." Except instead of singing "do-re-mi" they were singing nonsense rhymes. Andrew, who is shy and quiet, was sitting at the table with us, methodically eating his cereal.

"What's happening today?" I asked Nannie.

"Boo!" (Karen) "Ooh!" (David Michael) "Foo!" . . .

"Bowling," said Nannie, eyeing the plum preserves for seconds.

"They're good for bowling," I said helpfully.

"My thoughts exactly," she replied, reaching for them again. "What are you doing today?"

"Baby-sitting for David Michael and Karen and Andrew and Emily Michelle this morning. This afternoon I get to take care of Jamie and Lucy Newton."

"Sounds like a busy day," said Nannie.

"Noooo," said David Michael, and it didn't rhyme, and it didn't sound very happy.

I got up and gave my plate a quick rinse and put it in the dishwasher. "Sounds like I better get started."

In the den I found David Michael and Karen staring at one another. They'd stopped singing. They were standing eyeball to eyeball.

"Kristy?" That was Mom. I took another quick look at David Michael and Karen. They weren't moving or blinking, so I stepped into the hall.

Mom and Watson were on their way out. "We'll be back at noon," said Mom. "Emily Michelle is just waking up."

"I'll go get her."

"Thanks, dear." Mom and Watson hurried out the door. For a moment it was quiet. I knew Charlie and Sam had left early. That just left the six of us in the house, all peaceful and calm.

"You blinked!" shrieked Karen.

At about the same time I heard Emily Michelle. "Hiiiii?"

I stuck my head in the den. "Start over," I

said to Karen and David Michael.

"He blinked first!"

"Did not!"

"Did too!"

"Listen," I suggested. "Close your eyes, and see if you can catch each other peeking."

"That's silly," said Karen.

"Really," said David Michael.

"Lilly!" sang Karen.

David Michael grinned and took a deep breath. I took one of my own, checked on Andrew (still working on his cereal), and ran upstairs to get Emily Michelle.

After that, the morning went a little more smoothly. Emily Michelle doesn't talk a lot yet, but she's learning. She was very definite about how I made her peanut butter English muffin, for example, but in a nice, positive way. "Yes!" she crowed when I started making it. "Oh-oh!" she said, sounding very alarmed when I reached for the plum preserves. Then when I switched to the applesauce she beamed. "Yes!" she said again, happily.

The sun was shining outside, so after Emily had eaten, we all took Shannon out into the backyard.

Shannon's great. She's a Bernese mountain dog puppy, and she's enthusiastic about everything. She's still in her clumsy puppy stage, but she's very smart. And it's funny, she seems to understand that Emily Michelle is littler and more vulnerable than David Michael or Karen or Andrew. She's always much calmer with Emily.

Karen picked up a leaf as soon as we got outside and stuck it under her headband. "I'm a leaf collector," she said.

"Me, too," said David Michael.

"I'm the *chief* leaf collector. You are the executive vice-president in charge of choosing colors."

"Red," said David Michael instantly. They bent over and started searching for red leaves. Shannon and Andrew joined in, not sure what they were doing, but glad to help out.

"You want to make a leaf collection, Emily?" I asked.

Emily squatted down and peered at a leaf. She picked it up and looked it over with a serious expression. Then she put it back down exactly where she found it.

"No?" I asked.

She looked at me solemnly.

"We can write messages on the green leaves. Would you like to do that?" I pulled a couple of green leaves off of a tree and brought them back. I picked up a twig and wrote a big E on one. "See," I said. "That's an E. It's what your name begins with."

I handed it to her. She inspected it, then

put it down precisely, and looked at me expectantly.

"As leaf chief," said Karen, "I now declare we have all the red leaves in the whole yard."

"Hi," said a voice behind me just then and I looked up. "Shannon," I said. "Hi! Can you stay for awhile?"

Shannon Kilbourne lives across the street. When I first moved into the neighborhood, I thought she was an awful snob. But she's turned out to be a good friend, even though we don't get to see that much of each other. (Shannon goes to a private school.)

"Not right now," said Shannon. "Astrid and I are going for a walk, and we came to see if you wanted to come."

Just then Shannon the puppy saw her mother and frisked over to her. (Shannon gave us one of Astrid's puppies when our collie, Louie, died. We'll never forget Louie, but it's nice having a puppy around, too. And yes, David Michael named Shannon the puppy for Shannon the person.) The two dogs touched noses, tails wagging furiously.

"I wish I could go with you guys," I said, "but I'm baby-sitting."

"Yeah . . . I could put it off. What about this afternoon?"

"I have another job this afternoon," I said regretfully.

16

"Oh. Well, listen. Maybe tomorrow. Astrid needs the exercise. She's gaining weight, and that's not good."

"Her daughter could always use some leash practice."

"Okay. See you tomorrow maybe. Come on, Astrid." She pulled gently on Astrid's leash, and Astrid went along easily.

"See that?" I asked Shannon the puppy.

By the time the morning was over, we had collected a pile of yellow leaves, a pile of red leaves, a pile of red and yellow leaves, a pile of orange leaves, and a pile of brown ones. And I had helped Emily Michelle spell out her name in leaves.

"Now," said Karen. "We will do the leaf dance." She raised her hands and began skipping in and out among the piles. David Michael started doing a sort of bunny hop of his own after her.

"Leaf!" he shrieked.

"Chief," sang Karen.

"Beef," sang David Michael.

Then Shannon got in on the act. Woofing happily, she plunged after them. Only she didn't dance in and out among the piles of leaves. She jumped *into* the piles. The leaves went flying every which way.

"Oh, no!" cried David Michael.

"Good grief," I muttered. Karen put her

hands on her hips and frowned at Shannon. Shannon jumped up, trying to catch a leaf.

Then David Michael said, "It's a real leaf dance."

The frown left Karen's face. "It is. It is!"

She and David Michael followed Shannon, throwing leaves everywhere.

It really was a leaf dance, and fun to watch. David Michael and Karen and Andrew and Shannon were jumping and weaving around in all the colors.

"Come on," I said to Emily Michelle. "We have time for just one dance before lunch."

"Yes," replied Emily. She reached down and picked up her leaves in her fist. Then she and I walked over to the leaf dance.

David Michael was spinning in circles now, making himself dizzy. Karen joined in. Emily studied them for a moment, then smiled. She drew back her arm and threw her fist of leaves into the middle of the dance.

"Oh-oh," she said.

"Yes-yes," I said. "Let's dance." I danced Emily around in the leaves until she started to laugh. Then I felt someone watching. I looked up. It was Bart Taylor, sitting on his bike.

"Come on," I called to him.

Bart parked his bike and stepped to the edge of the leaf dance.

"Hi," I said. I indicated swirls of leaves and the children. "Leaf dance," I explained.

"Looks like fun," he said, and I knew he meant it. He didn't act like it was childish or weird to find me covered with leaves. It's one of the things I like about Bart — in addition to his deep, deep brown eyes and nice smile and . . . anyway.

"It is fun," I said. "Want to join us?"

"I just stopped by to say hello," he said. "I'm on my way to a Bashers practice in a little while."

"How're they doing?" I asked.

He raised his eyebrows at me. "Want to come scout?" he asked.

"Maybe later," I said. "I've got another job this afternoon."

"Okay," he answered. We watched the leaf dance for a little while longer; then Bart had to go. "Come by if you can," he said. I waved as he rode his bike away. I knew I probably wouldn't be able to make it. I had homework, for one thing — especially some serious science studying to do.

Mom and Watson came home not too much later, and we ate lunch. Karen kept her chief's leaf on, and at lunch Emily Michelle looked up, then said, distinctly, "Leaf."

"Good for you," said Watson.

"Next time," said Karen, "you can be leaf chief, Emily. *I* will be . . ."

But I didn't get to hear what she'd be. "Oh, my lord," I exclaimed. "I've got to get over to the Newtons'. See you later."

I got to the Newtons' just in time. Jamie, who is four going on five, answered the door with his mother.

"Hi, Jamie. Hi, Mrs. Newton."

"Kristy, come on in." Baby-sitting for the Newtons is one of my favorite jobs, not just because Jamie is fun and funny, or because his baby sister, Lucy, is adorable. Mrs. Newton is also very well organized. She had written down where she could be for the next couple of hours, and had left snacks for Jamie in the refrigerator.

"You know where everything is," she said as she was going out. "Lucy should sleep. I'll be back by five."

Jamie and I waved to her, and then Jamie led me into the living room. He stopped by the window and stood staring out.

"Jamie?" I said. It wasn't like him to act upset when his mother left. He usually liked having me baby-sit for him.

He didn't answer. "Jamie, she'll be back at five o'clock. Now, let's see what we — "

"Look," breathed Jamie.

I looked. A group of boys Jamie's age and

a little older were pedaling their bicycles frantically down the sidewalk. "You want to go out and ride your trike with them?"

But Jamie shook his head vigorously. Then he looked at me, his eyes shining. "Not yet, Kristy," he said.

He waited, so I asked him, "When, then?"

"When I get my bike." He started hopping in place, he was so excited. "Guess what, guess what, guess what," he sang.

It looked like it was my day for singing baby-sitting charges.

"What?" I asked.

"*I'm* getting a *real* bicycle."

"Wow . . . a real bicycle."

"NOT a tricycle. A bicycle."

"That's great, Jamie."

"And I'll be able to go fast and faster and faster!"

I put my hand on his shoulder and spoke slowly before he went any faster. "That really is good news, Jamie. I remember when I got my first bicycle."

"You do? Was learning to ride hard?"

I thought about it. I didn't remember it being hard, but I didn't want to tell Jamie it was too easy, in case he didn't pick it up right away.

"Not hard, exactly," I said. "Besides, it's just like playing softball for the Krushers. With practice, you can do it."

"I'm going to practice and practice and practice."

"How about if we do something else right now."

"Can we read a book?"

"You pick one out and we will. First let me go and check on Lucy." Jamie headed for his room, and I went to Lucy's.

She was sleeping like a baby. I wanted to pick her up, she's so soft and sweet smelling (most of the time, anyway) and fun to hold. But I knew if I woke her up and she didn't go back to sleep it would mean she might be cranky later on. And I didn't think Mrs. Newton would be happy with a sitter who left cranky babies in her wake.

"Kristy!" called Jamie.

I went to his room and settled down on the bed next to him. "Okay, what book did you pick out?"

"It's a new one," he said. He held it up and I read the title: *The Bicycle Rider*.

Those bicycle wheels must have still been spinning in my head when Stacey called that night after I finally settled in to do some homework.

"Listen, Kristy, I've been thinking," she said.

"And I've been trying to," I said. "But vertebrates are *not* something my brain likes to dwell on."

"Well, what about this, then? Have you made up your mind about running for class president?"

"You think it's a good idea?" I asked. This was much more interesting than science homework.

"Who's more organized than you are?" asked Stacey. "And you're the president of the Baby-sitters Club, so you have experience. Somebody needs to do something about the school, and not just the lunches."

"We-e-ll," I said. "Let me think about it a little more."

"You might think about this, too," said Stacey. "I heard Grace Blume is running." (She's one of Cokie's cronies.)

"I'll let you know Monday."

"Good," replied Stacey.

And that's what I thought about for the rest of the weekend — when I had the time.

CHAPTER 3

The first thing Claudia said when I reached her house for the meeting Monday afternoon was, "Have you made up your mind yet?" So I knew she and Stacey had been talking it over. I'd been talking it over too, sort of — with myself. But I still wanted to talk about it a little more with the others.

I shook my head and settled into the director's chair, pulling the visor I usually wear down low. "Okay," said Claudia cheerfully. She began rummaging behind her dresser, and I knew she was looking for something to eat.

Claudia is a junk-food fanatic, and she keeps goodies stashed all over her room in places she doesn't even remember, sometimes. Her room is sort of a secret junk-food collage, if you think about it. She's very creative about collecting junk food, hiding it, and finding it.

Her ambition is to be an artist, and she is really good. She once got an honorable mention in a show at a local art gallery for a work in progress (she would have gotten first place if the piece had been finished). But she doesn't like school very much. She's a terrible speller, for example.

Maybe part of it is that her sister, Janine, is a real genius. She's still in high school, but she's already taking college courses, and when she talks, she's very formal. She's a conservative dresser, too. Not at all like Claudia.

Today, for instance, Claudia was wearing lime green bicycle pants, a long, long bright pink shirt, and a cropped lime green striped shirt over that. She was also wearing black hightop leather sneakers with pink butterfly barrettes clipped to the laces. She had two feather earrings in one ear (lime green, of course), and a tiny pink heart in the other. Claudia's gorgeous — she has perfect skin and she's Japanese-American, with dark eyes and shining black hair (today it was pulled up on top of her head and fell down to one side). But even so, not many gorgeous people could get away with some of the outfits Claudia pulls together. But that's how she always looks. Pulled together and gorgeous.

Claudia is the vice-president of the Babysitters Club because we meet in her room three times a week on Monday, Wednesday, and Friday, from 5:30 until 6:00. Claudia has her own private phone line, the only one of us who does. This is good because when we use the phone, we don't tie it up for the other people in her family.

I'm the president since I thought of the idea for the BSC. I got it one night while I was listening to my mother call around, trying to find a baby-sitter for David Michael. Suddenly, it came to me. What if Mom could make one phone call and reach several different baby-sitters at once? Actually, I thought, reach three baby-sitters at once, since Mary Anne and Claudia and I were already doing a lot of baby-sitting. But we agreed that three might not be enough, so Claudia suggested that Stacey join us. Stacey had just moved to Stoneybrook and was starting to be friends with Claudia.

She said yes. So with Mary Anne as secretary and Stacey as treasurer, we were all set. We advertised and worked hard, and we got good recommendations. Soon we had all the baby-sitting jobs we could handle.

That's when Mary Anne suggested we ask Dawn, who'd just moved to Stoneybrook from California, if she'd like to be a member of the club, too. Dawn agreed, and she became our alternate officer. Then Stacey had to move back to New York (it turned out to be temporary), and we still had as much business as before, if not more, so Jessi Ramsey and Mallory Pike joined us as junior officers. In fact, everybody in the club is an officer except Logan and Shannon, who are associate members. They help us out when we need extra baby-sitters.

Mary Anne, who is my best friend, and Dawn, who is Mary Anne's other best friend, arrived at the meeting next. They came in the door, just as Claudia shrieked, "Aha!"

Mary Anne stopped, looking a little flustered. Then she saw the sweet 'n' sour gummy bears Claudia was holding up and smiled.

"Catch," Claudia said, and tossed the bag to Mary Anne. Then she got down on her knees and started running her hand between the mattress and the boxsprings of her bed.

"Thank you," said Mary Anne. She sat cross-legged on the bed, opened the club notebook, and put the gummy bears beside her. Dawn sat down opposite her in Claud's desk chair.

I guess the fact that Mary Anne and I are best friends proves that opposites attract. We do look sort of alike. We both have brown hair and brown eyes and are short. Actually, I'm the shortest person in our class. But where I have a big mouth and sometimes say things without thinking, Mary Anne is quiet and shy. She even dressed like a shy kid, until she convinced her father to let her grow up a little.

Her father couldn't help being strict. Mary Anne's mother had died when Mary Anne was very young, and Mr. Spier wanted to make sure he raised Mary Anne right. But he was very hard on her. Now she pays more attention to clothes, although her style is very different from Claudia's or Stacey's, and she wears her hair in distinctive styles. That's another way in which Mary Anne and I are different. I'm happy just wearing jeans and a T-shirt or a turtleneck, and running shoes. In cold weather, I just add a sweater and sometimes a baseball cap. My best baseball cap has a collie on it. That's in memory of Louie. He got very sick and we had to have him put to sleep. (It was Louie, in a way who helped Shannon and me to become friends.) I like my hair to look casual, too.

Mary Anne is also very sensitive and romantic. Maybe because of that, she's the first one of us to have a real boyfriend. That's Logan Bruno. He's a Southerner, and Mary Anne thinks he looks just like Cam Geary, her favorite star. And even though I'm not interested in boys much (except for Bart Taylor), Logan *is* cute.

Anyway, Mary Anne's father not only started letting Mary Anne make some changes, he did some major changing himself. He got *married*. He married Dawn's mother,

Mrs. Schafer! Only she's Mrs. Spier, now. They'd known each other in high school here in Stoneybrook, when Dawn's mom was Sharon Porter. But things hadn't worked out and Dawn's mother moved to California and married Dawn's dad. The Schafers had Dawn and Dawn's brother, Jeff, but then they got divorced. And Mrs. Schafer ended up back in Stoneybrook. That's how Mary Anne went from being an only child, except for her kitten, Tigger, to having a good-sized family. The Schafers and Spiers live in Dawn's house, now, since it's bigger. And Dawn is now not only Mary Anne's other best friend, but her sister, too.

Once you see Dawn, you never forget her. She is striking looking. She has long, long, pale, pale blonde hair, blue eyes, and is tall and slender. And she definitely has her own personal style — like the two holes pierced in each earlobe. Plus, she will *not* eat junk food. Or red meat. But she will eat tofu. And real, *live* fruit. I mean an apple is okay, but it's not my first choice.

Other than that Dawn is very easygoing. She does her own thing, and lets people do theirs. It's hard to shake Dawn up, although she does get hurt. She's been through some tough times, too. Not only did her parents get divorced and her mother move back to Stoneybrook (and away from the warm California sun), but in the end, Dawn's little brother, Jeff, decided to move back to California to live with his father. Dawn had thought about living in California, too, once, but fortunately for us she decided to stay. And now, after adjusting to her new life with Richard (Mr. Spier) and Mary Anne, I think Dawn's perfectly happy in Stoneybrook.

Oh, yes. Dawn loves ghost stories. And the old farmhouse she lives in *might be haunted.* We've never been able to prove it is. But we've never been able to prove it isn't, either. At least there's a secret passage in it that might be haunted.

"Aha!" said Claudia again. She tossed a bag of pretzels to Dawn, and propped herself against the headboard of the bed, holding a bag of double-dipped chocolate Oreos.

Stacey, Jessi, and Mal were the last to arrive at the meeting.

You already know a little about Stacey. What you don't know is that in addition to being New York sharp (and cool), Stacey is also a diabetic. That's a disease in which your pancreas doesn't make enough insulin, which means your blood sugar level can get out of control. When that happens you could faint, or even get really sick. So Stacey has to give herself injections of insulin every day and watch what she eats very strictly. Absolutely no sugar. In a way, she has the same problem with her parents that Mary Anne had with her father. Stacey's an only child, too, and when her parents found out she was diabetic, they started being super, super cautious and careful with her. They also started taking her to all different kinds of doctors, even when Stacey finally felt that she was handling things and had a doctor she liked and knew was doing a good job. Stacey had to talk pretty firmly to her parents, too, but at last they understood.

Anyway, Anastasia Elizabeth McGill (that's Stacey's real name, but don't call her that!) moved to Stoneybrook in seventh grade when her father's company transferred him to Stamford. Then, just a year later, they transferred him back to New York. So Stacey returned to the town she was born and raised in — but not for long. Stacey's parents got divorced, and her mother moved back to Stoneybrook. And Stacey chose to come back to Connecticut, too.

Stacey is boy-crazy (just like Claudia). She is also a way cool dresser. Like that Monday, she was wearing a black skirt and tights that were two colors: one leg was red and the other was black. And her shoes were shiny black and laced up to the ankles. She was also wearing this enormous black turtleneck sweater with red flecks in it, and one round red earring and one square black one. Her hair, which was in a mid-perm stage around her face, was pulled back with this silver lamé band.

She looked smashing.

Jessi Ramsey and Mallory Pike are both eleven years old, in sixth grade, and best friends. Mal used to be one of our baby-sitting charges. She's from a family of eight kids (she has four brothers, three of them identical triplets, and three sisters), so she's had a lot of experience with children. It was only natural that she "graduate" to being a member of the BSC herself. And Jessi is sort of connected to Stacey. When Stacey moved back to New York, Jessi's family moved into Stacey's old house.

Jessi and Mallory are two very different best friends (like me and Mary Anne) who also have a lot in common. They're both the oldest in their families, and their families still treat them like babies (at least, that's the way Mal and Jessi feel). But they did manage to get pierced ears. And they both love horse stories, particularly Marguerite Henry's stories. Oh, yes — they both have pet hamsters.

Mal wears glasses and has braces and red hair. She likes to draw and write and would like to be a children's book writer and illustrator someday.

Jessi's family is a good bit smaller than Mal's — average size, with her parents, her aunt Cecelia, an eight-year-old sister named Becca, and a baby brother named Squirt. And her passion is ballet. She's good, too. She takes special classes at a dance school in Stamford, where you have to audition just to get in. She's already danced lead roles in performances before hundreds of people.

Another difference is that Jessi doesn't have braces or glasses or red hair. She is black, with black hair and brown eyes. This doesn't matter to Mal or to any of us, but some people in Stoneybrook, I am ashamed to say, were bothered. The Ramseys' neighbors gave them a hard time in the beginning. Luckily, they've settled down now.

And that's the Baby-sitters Club. I looked around at everyone and cleared my throat. It was exactly 5:30. "The meeting will come to order," I said.

"See? You even talk like a class president," Stacey pointed out.

Just then the phone rang. I picked it up. "Hello, Baby-sitters Club."

It was Mrs. Newton. I took down the information about the sitter she needed and told her I'd call her right back.

"Mrs. Newton needs someone next Monday from three-thirty until five. She's taking Lucy

33

to the pediatrician for a checkup."

Mary Anne flipped the club notebook open.

"Stacey, you're already scheduled for the Marshalls. And Mal, you and Jessi are down for — "

"I know. My family." Mal's mother always wants more than one baby-sitter because those seven kids are definitely a handful.

"I've got an art class," Claudia said.

"Krusher practice," I said, reluctantly. Jamie is one of my favorite baby-sitting charges, and we're all crazy about Lucy, too.

"That leaves Dawn and me," said Mary Anne. "Dawn, if you'd rather — "

"No. You take it, Mary Anne. I need some free time, and a Monday is good for that."

"Don't forget our BSC meeting," I pointed out.

Dawn flashed a smile at me. "How could I forget?"

The phone rang again, and Mary Anne picked it up. It was the Papadakises, who live in my neighborhood. After we'd arranged for a sitter — Dawn this time — we had a lull.

"Did you see the notice about the class play?" asked Claud. She was alternately eating Oreos and sweet 'n' sour gummy bears. It made me go all pucker-mouthed just to watch.

"*Mary Poppins*," I said. "Disgusting."

"I used to love *Mary Poppins*," said Mary Anne diplomatically.

"*Used to* is the operative phrase here. I can't believe it! I think we should do something *real*."

"Definitely," said Dawn. "*Mary Poppins* is a little babyish. Now if it was *A Raisin in the Sun.* . . ."

"Or what about *Our Town*? Or *The Glass Menagerie*? I mean, why don't we have any say in this? School is supposed to be challenging! Not . . . not Mary Poppinsish!" I said.

"Well, I just want to work on the scenery. Maybe you could do it, too, Mal?" Claudia put in.

"You know," I said, really working up steam. "The play committee could use the talent we have at SMS, too. Like Jessi — "

Jessi laughed. "This sounds like a speech, Kristy."

"Yeah," said Stacey. "A candidate's speech."

I stopped. "You honestly think I should run?"

"You should do what you *want* to do," Mary Anne said firmly.

Was Mary Anne trying to tell me something? If she was, I wasn't listening. At least not then.

I looked around the room. If I ran, I would

have a head start. I had Team Kristy right there — the Baby-sitters Club. I knew I could count on my friends.

"I'll do it," I said. "I hearby officially announce my candidacy for class president."

"All right!" cried Stacey.

"Awesome," said Dawn.

"That's great, Kristy," said Mal.

"Dues and treasurer's report, please," I said suddenly to Stacey, switching back to the BSC meeting. I'd had so much to think about, I'd almost forgotten.

We all groaned, but we each handed over our dollar apiece. "That makes us seven dollars richer," reported Stacey. "We *were* getting low," she said after giving us the grand total.

The phone rang. As Mary Anne answered, Mal looked around at us.

"I was thinking of running for office, too," said Mal. "For secretary of the sixth grade."

"Way to go," I said, but I have to admit, I was thinking more about my own campaign.

Mal went on. "I don't know. Maybe not. Probably no one would vote for me."

"You have my vote," said Jessi.

"You'll do great, Mal," said Mary Anne loyally.

Mal blushed a little, but she didn't look entirely convinced.

I glanced at my watch. It was 6:00. "Uh-oh.

Time to go. Charlie will be here any minute to pick me up. (We pay him out of our dues to drive me to and from BSC meetings.)

"Kristy for president!" sang out Claudia.

I had to admit, it sounded pretty good.

CHAPTER 4

Jamie was excited. And that's an understatement.

"Do you see anything?" he asked me for about the thousandth time.

"Not yet," I said.

Today was the day his bike was being delivered. There was a good chance it would arrive before his mother returned from her meeting. I hoped so. Jamie's enthusiasm was contagious. I was excited myself.

Jamie went down to the end of the driveway and peered both ways. He came back. "I don't see anything yet."

"A watched pot never boils, Jamie."

Jamie wrinkled his nose. "What does that mean?"

That stopped me. I'd heard it all my life, but I'd never explained it to anyone. "It means, well, it means that if you keep looking for something to happen, it's not going to. Like if you were watching a pot of water, waiting for it to boil, it would never boil. Or it would *seem* like it was never going to, because all you were doing was standing there watching it."

Jamie looked even more confused than I sounded. Luckily, just then I heard Lucy through the open front door of the house.

"Come on," I said.

Jamie followed me reluctantly into the house, looking back over his shoulder every step of the way. I would have let him stay outside, but I didn't want him racing out to the street to watch for the bike while I wasn't with him.

"We'll go back outside," I promised. "You can help pick out a toy for Lucy to play with."

"She likes anything," said Jamie. But he came along behind me.

Lucy is the *best* baby. She is sooo cute. And smart. She'd just let out one little experimental sort of wail, to get my attention. When I got to her room she was making urgley-smiling sounds.

"Urgley-urgley to you." I smiled at her and reached down and picked her up to check if she needed changing. Fortunately, she didn't.

Jamie picked up a soft bright cloth bunny with embroidered eyes and long embroidered eyelashes.

"Hurry," he said.

We'd just reached the front hall when we heard the sound of the truck pulling up.

"My bike's here!" Jamie screeched, and he took off.

Sure enough, the delivery man was lifting a big box out of the back of the truck.

"Newtons'?" he asked.

"I'm Jamie Newton," Jamie told him. "That's *my* bike."

I signed for the bike, and settled Lucy in her playpen in the yard while Jamie wrestled with the cardboard.

We peeled the bike free and stepped back to admire it. Only it almost fell over. Jamie's face fell. "It's supposed to have training wheels."

"Wait a minute. It does. Look, here they are, wrapped separately." I studied the sheet of instructions that had come with the bike. "It looks like all you have to do is screw them on."

Jamie didn't seem any happier. "I don't know *how*."

"Neither do I, but we can try. You have some tools in that drawer in the kitchen, remember? Go in and get a screwdriver and a pair of pliers. Okay?"

"Please," Jamie reminded me.

"Please," I added, and he ran toward the kitchen. While he was gone, I stuffed the cardboard packaging into the recycling bin and took another look at the instructions. No problem. I hoped.

And it wasn't. Maybe I should take mechanics or something, because the wheels went on as easy as could be. There was even a little tube of grease for the wheels and the chain.

"All set. Ready to roll, Jamie?"

Jamie was so excited he'd stopped talking. He just nodded vigorously.

"Okay. Up you go." I gave him a boost and rolled the bicycle across the patch of grass onto the driveway.

But when I looked at Jamie again, he wasn't smiling. He was just staring down at the ground.

"Jamie? Ready for your first real bike trip?"

Jamie didn't nod. Instead he shook his head, still looking at the ground.

"What's wrong?" I asked.

He looked up then. "I'm going to fall," he wailed. "I'm going to fall and it's going to hurt!" He stared back down at the ground.

"Oh, Jamie." I put an arm behind him. "No you won't. You have the extra wheels, see? You're all balanced. You won't fall. I'll stay right with you." Jamie didn't answer. But I could feel how tense he was. "We could wait. Just a little while, you know. Until you got used to the idea."

"NO."

I waited, anyway. This was a new one. I tried to think what to do, tried to remember learning to ride a bike myself. And come to think of it I *did* remember falling. But that was after the training wheels, wasn't it?

While we were standing in a frozen tableau in the driveway, Claudia showed up. "Claudia!" Was I ever relieved. Two heads would be better than one for sure.

"Hi, Kristy. Hi, Jamie. Neat bike!"

Jamie smiled and looked up (just for a second). "It's mine."

"I know. You look great." Jamie nodded slightly.

"So, Claudia. Why don't you get on the other side and we'll walk alongside Jamie and hold onto him and the bike for his first ride," I suggested. "Sort of like human training wheels."

Claud understood right away. "Great." She put her arm around Jamie and gave him a little squeeze. "Let's just take a couple of steps, for practice, okay?"

Jamie nodded a little more, so that's what we did. Two steps, stop, then two more steps, stop, then two more.

"Don't you have art class today?" I asked Claud.

"Got out early. Mary Anne said you were here today, so I came over." We reached the end of the driveway and made a big wide half-circle turn and started back. Jamie was frowning with concentration.

"Because," Claudia went on, "I have some ideas for your campaign."

"The campaign? Oh — great!" I hadn't forgotten about it. I mean, who could, when you'd had to register and fill out forms and all that at school. But I'd sort of put it off, because no one could officially start campaigning till the following week.

Which wasn't that far away now.

"What I thought is, you need a theme. And a striking design. But something simple, too. That's the key to good design, you know. Simplicity. A shape the eye can instantly recognize as symbolic of what, or who, it represents." Claudia may not like school, but she knows art.

We reached the top of the driveway and

waited while Claudia flipped through her art notebook. "Here," she said, holding something out to me.

On a piece of paper was the letter "K," a really standout drawing of it. By the top of it was a + sign. "See," Claudia explained. "It can mean K+ like a super grade in school. And what we do is we put this everywhere: You could just go around putting the word *Okay* everywhere, but with your brand-name K+ in it."

"That's how you really spell it, isn't it?" I teased, and Claudia who is a world-class creative speller — which unfortunately means she doesn't always spell words the way the dictionary does — grinned.

I grinned, too. "It looks great, Claudia." I was really getting psyched now. "We can make buttons and all kinds of slogans — "

"Like A+ = K+."

"Or *Extra*-special K."

"Or Kristy for K+ President," said Claudia, writing it out quickly in her notebook.

"It's definitely time to get organized. Maybe we could get together after the club meets this Friday. I don't have a sitting job that night, and we can check with Mary Anne and see who does — "

"Even if they do, we could have pizza and just go to our jobs from my house."

"Good idea. Claudia, you're a genius."

Claudia looked pleased.

Jamie, meanwhile, did not. "More," he said. "I need to practice more."

I checked on Lucy, who was still being the perfect baby, crawling contentedly around the playpen. "Hi, Lucy," I said. She sat up and waved her hands around, making a sound that could have meant "Hi, Kristy."

"Kristy!"

"Coming, Jamie!" I patted Lucy gently, then went back and took up my position by the bike.

As we turned and headed down the driveway again, Claudia said, "Oh, I almost forgot. Mal's decided to go ahead and run for secretary of the sixth grade. Jessi's going to manage her campaign."

"She'll do a great job," I said. "Will you be my campaign manager?"

"We-e-ell," said Claudia, pretending to think. "Since I *am* an artistic genius, I suppose I can."

"Super. Super-plus," I said.

"Kristy for president." Claudia flung up her free hand and pretended she was waving to a crowd.

"Baby-sitters rule," I answered, laughing.

We pushed Jamie up and down the drive way about a hundred more times until his mother came home. I thought he was getting better, but I couldn't be sure. At least we weren't stopping every two steps. I was glad I hadn't told him that learning to ride a bike was easy. Right now it looked like Jamie was going to have to work pretty hard at it, even with training wheels.

But I knew he would, too. That's one of the things I like about Jamie, that we all like. He's definitely not a quitter.

CHAPTER 5

At the end of our meeting on Friday, as Mal and Jessi were heading down the stairs to go sit for Mal's brothers and sisters, I got out of the director's chair and indicated that Claud should sit in it.

"You're the campaign manager," I said.

"Speech, speech," teased Stacey.

Claudia held up the bag of taco chips she'd been devouring and said, "I hereby declare as my first official act as Kristy's campaign manager that we order pizza."

"We *do* have to keep up our strength," Dawn put in. "Good nutrition is a key ingredient to a successful campaign . . . I vote for 'shrooms."

"Onions," said Stacey.

"Double cheese," Mary Anne said.

"Pepperoni?" I asked. "On half," I added as Dawn wrinkled her nose.

Claudia pulled the phone toward her and

placed the order, while Mary Anne turned to me. "Do you want me to collect money from everyone, or . . ."

Like a good baby-sitter — and a good candidate for class president — I was prepared. "We can't use the BSC money, of course. So this is on me. Think of it as campaign expenses."

"I can see you know how to campaign," said Dawn solemnly.

"I also know how to shake hands, and I'm *very* good at kissing babies."

Stacey said, "You've got to win, Kristy. Look at the other candidates. Alan Gray . . ."

"Yeah, but he nominated himself," said Dawn reasonably. "He's probably not going to get all that many votes."

"Besides, Alan Gray would probably shake babies and kiss hands," I said, choking. The thought of Alan Gray kissing *anybody* made me shudder.

"And then Grace," said Dawn. "She definitely got nominated."

Grace Blume wasn't a much better candidate in my opinion. After all, she, like Cokie, has pulled some nasty tricks on me and the others in the BSC. Still, she's popular, which is probably why she's running. For Grace, being elected to class president means winning a popularity contest, and that's about it. She'd probably just rest on her laurels — after she'd gotten a rule passed against members of the Baby-sitters Club attending Stoneybrook Middle School!

"Pete Black got nominated, too. He's not so bad," Mary Anne said.

I wrinkled my nose. I didn't want to contradict Mary Anne, but I think Pete can be really immature.

Mary Anne saw me and smiled. "But you're definitely the best, Kristy."

"Right on," said Dawn.

"Right on?" asked Stacey.

"I think it's an old hippie expression."

"Oh. Like far out."

"Like right." Dawn shook back her blonde hair, which she had fixed in little braids around her face.

"Like the pizza won't be here for at least twenty minutes, so let's get started," said Claudia, hanging up the phone. She flipped open her art notebook. She'd done a new, more detailed drawing of some of the K+ designs. They really stood out.

"I thought we'd use this design for our handouts, and we can try other designs for the posters. Mary Anne, did you bring poster paper?"

"Didn't you see me bring it in?" Mary Anne motioned to where a huge bag of poster paper was propped against the foot of the bed.

"Right," said Claudia, very officially. "Now, we can also make buttons, like this . . ." She flashed another design ". . . or this."

Mary Anne reached out for the designs and studied them thoughtfully. "I like them both."

Claudia nodded. "Well, we could use them both . . ."

"Whichever we choose, we can't do that right away," said Stacey, being practical. "To make buttons we need dozens and dozens of the same design."

"You're right, Stace. I need to make a whole sheet of designs, and then we can do color Xeroxes of the sheet and cut the designs out. That'll save time."

"And meanwhile we can start on the posters. And if we don't finish them this afternoon, I can ask David Michael to help me finish them at home."

Claudia started pulling out newspapers to spread around on the floor, and paint and Magic Markers, and soon we were making posters while Claud concentrated on the sheet of button designs.

We worked for awhile, and just as I was beginning to think seriously about pizza, there was a knock on the door. Claudia opened it to find her sister, Janine.

Standing next to each other, Claudia and

Janine couldn't have looked more different, even though that day Claudia was dressed fairly conservatively: white jeans, red shoes with big bows, a tropical jungle shirt with each button shaped like a piece of fruit, and her hair pulled to one side over her shoulder with a banana barrette. But Janine, with her short hair and bangs, her pullover sweater, and plain skirt and loafers, made Claudia look extremely exotic.

"I believe you would be glad to know that a pizza delivery has just been effected," said Janine. She talks like that all the time. It's part of being a genius.

"Right," said Claudia. I got up, pulling the money out of my pocket, and ran downstairs with her.

When we got back upstairs, carrying the pizza and balancing napkins and plates and Diet Cokes, Janine had stepped into the room and was studying the posters we'd finished and propped against one wall to dry.

"You've chosen a logo, I see." She peered over her glasses more closely at one of them. "It's quite a good one. Simple, but striking. That's extremely important in product identification. The consumer has to be able to make the association readily between the identifying symbol and what it represents."

Normally, Janine's encyclopedia act, even

though she doesn't mean to sound so formal, can be a little trying. But this time I just stopped and stared. "You know what, Janine? That's exactly, or *almost* exactly what Claudia said!"

Claudia and Janine looked at each other, and then we all burst out laughing.

"Well," said Janine, turning to go, "I can see your campaign is in excellent hands, Kristy. I wish you the best of luck."

"You said it!" I gave Janine the two thumbs-up sign.

"Thanks, Janine," said Claudia, sounding a little surprised. It's hard to admit, because older siblings can be a pain sometimes, but getting a compliment from them is extra special. And Janine is not someone to just throw compliments around.

Which made me more sure than ever that I had the best possible campaign manager. And team. But would that mean I would win the election?

Chewing on a slice of pepperoni pizza, I looked around. Stacey, as cool as ever, eating a slice of double cheese, pepperoni, onion, and mushroom pizza; Claudia, who was absently picking the mushrooms off her slice and studying her art notebook; Dawn, laughing and trying to catch the strings of cheese with her fingers; and Mary Anne, carefully taking small bites of her pizza and grinning at Dawn. I grinned myself. With the Baby-sitters Club behind me, how could I lose?

But then I remembered Grace the Snob, who probably thought a good class president was the one who was the leader of a very select group of total snobs; and Alan, the Pest of All the World (whose principle qualification for leadership, as far as I could tell, had been leading half the school off into the distance during the fire drill); and That Nerd Pete, and I stopped grinning. I had to win, I *had* to. I was not being arrogant. I simply knew how important it was for me to be elected. Because if I wasn't, look at the remaining choices.

I had to run, and I had to win, and I had to do it to save the eighth grade.

CHAPTER 6

Friday

Well, Kristy and Claudia had told us how excited Jamie Newton is about his new bicycle. They'd also told us he seemed a little unsure of him- self. That's not surprising. I remember I was, too. (I can really remember that, as well as the first time I rode without my father helping. It was great.) But I don't know how we're going to get Jamie sure enough of himself to take that first big step. Or pedal....

When Mary Anne arrived at Jamie's that afternoon, Jamie, Mrs. Newton, *and* Lucy met her.

"Terrific," said Mrs. Newton. "Right on time, as always."

Mary Anne thought that was a good beginning, even though Jamie shot past Mary Anne without even saying hello.

"Hi, Mrs. Newton. Hi, Lucy. Hi, Jamie," Mary Anne replied politely.

Mrs. Newton picked up her purse and Lucy's baby supplies tote, and headed toward her car. Mary Anne put down the Kid-Kit she'd brought along (not that she was going to get to use it!), and followed Mrs. Newton and Lucy. "Lucy's doctor is very good about not keeping her patients waiting, so we shouldn't be gone more than an hour and a half. Jamie can have a snack in an hour, but not any later than that. I don't want him to spoil his dinner."

"Good luck," said Mary Anne.

"Come on!" That was Jamie, shouting from the driveway, where he'd wheeled his bicycle out of the garage.

"It's just a routine checkup," Mrs. Newton reassured Mary Anne, putting Lucy into her car seat. After they'd backed out of the driveway and driven away, Mary Anne trotted over to Jamie, who was still holding onto the handlebars of his bicycle.

"It's a beautiful bicycle, Jamie. Did you choose the color yourself?"

"Yes," said Jamie. Mary Anne could tell how preoccupied he was, because normally he would have told her all about why he'd chosen red with white racing stripes and at least a dozen other wonderful things about whatever it was that interested him — which in this case, of course, was his bike.

But he wasn't interested in talking about his bike that day. He was interested in riding it.

"Hold on," he commanded.

"Hold on, please," said Mary Anne.

"Please," repeated Jamie shortly, and he began climbing onto the bike as Mary Anne held onto the handlebars.

"Are you going to show me how you ride?" she asked.

"No!" said Jamie. "I *just* got my bicycle. I don't know how to ride yet."

"Of course. Let's practice, then, okay?"

Since that was exactly what Jamie wanted, he didn't wait for an answer. He just started pedaling determinedly. When they reached the foot of the driveway, he slowed down almost to a stop. Mary Anne looked at him and saw that his face was red and he was biting his lower lip.

"You're doing a great job, Jamie," she said, half worried he was going to bite a hole in his lip.

They inched around the corner of the driveway and onto the sidewalk and Jamie didn't answer.

"Jamie?" said Mary Anne.

"Uh," grunted Jamie, but at least he stopped biting his lip. Mary Anne was surprised. She'd never seen Jamie quite like this. He's stubborn, but he's not obsessive or anything.

She was in for a bigger surprise when Jamie pedaled onto the sidewalk. He slowed down almost to a standstill for *every* crack. And when they reached the corner and had to turn around, Jamie slid off the bike.

"Are you tired?" asked Mary Anne.

"I'm *turning* around," replied Jamie, as if that should be obvious to anyone.

So Mary Anne helped Jamie turn the bike around and waited for him to climb back on, and they started down the sidewalk. They inched along in front of his house toward the corner at the other end of the block. Suddenly, Jamie came to a dead stop.

Mary Anne didn't ask if he was tired this time. She was learning. "What is it, Jamie?"

He pointed and shook his head violently. "That stick!"

Mary Anne looked and almost asked, "What

stick?" but, fortunately, she saw the skinny little stick lying on the sidewalk just in time.

"Do you want it?" she asked, and then realized the answer just as Jamie said, "It has to move!" If the cracks in the sidewalk scared him, then the stick probably seemed like a major obstacle.

But when Mary Anne let go of the bicycle to get the stick, Jamie howled, "DON'T!"

She waited for a moment for him to calm down, and then she said, "But, Jamie, how am I going to get the stick?"

He shook his head again without answering.

"Listen, Jamie," said Mary Anne patiently. "If you don't pedal and you don't move, you'll be perfectly fine. And I'll move the stick really fast. It'll only take a second. I promise."

Jamie hesitated, then said, "You *promise* promise?"

"Promise, promise, promise with a capital P," answered Mary Anne.

So Jamie made himself very rigid and straight and said, "Okay." Mary Anne grabbed the stick, threw it on the grass, and went back to Jamie.

He relaxed as she took hold of the bicycle again.

"See," said Mary Anne. "You did great. Wasn't that easy?" They started forward again and she said, "You know, you *have* made progress, Jamie. Didn't you need both Kristy and Claudia to help you ride the first day you got your bicycle?"

"Uh-huh," said Jamie. They came to the corner and he got off and turned the bike around and got back on.

Cheerfully, Mary Anne kept up a flow of encouraging conversation. "You know, everything gets easier with practice. You learned that from playing for the Krushers. Remember how hard it was for you when you started playing? Now Kristy and the Krushers wouldn't know what to do without you."

"Yeah," said Jamie, and he didn't sound quite so fearful. But he continued to slow down at every crack.

Encouraged, Mary Anne went on. "You know, it's like they say. If you're riding a horse and you fall off, the important thing is to get right back on."

Big mistake. Jamie's face turned bright red, and he practically screamed, "I'm not going to fall!"

By the time Mary Anne had calmed him down, they'd reached the foot of the driveway. "This is a lot of practice," she said. "Sometimes you can practice better if you take a break. Why don't we go get the Kid-Kit, and — "

"No."

"No, thank you," said Mary Anne, suppressing a sigh. The Kid-Kits are something all the kids love, because what kid doesn't like reading books that aren't his own, and playing with toys that aren't the same old ones. So we take our Kid-Kits to some of our jobs (not to all of them, because then they'd be ordinary, and not a treat) and replenish them with new toys and books and coloring books out of our dues from time to time.

Anyway, when Jamie said no to the Kid-Kit Mary Anne knew she was in for a really long afternoon with the bicycle.

"No, thank you," repeated Jamie, and then he stopped so abruptly that Mary Anne almost fell herself.

"You're good with the brakes," she said, but Jamie didn't hear her. He was staring at the sidewalk.

Mary Anne looked. All she saw was a leaf.

"The leaf?" she asked.

Jamie nodded.

She moved the leaf and they crept forward.

Every time she suggested they stop, Jamie refused. He didn't even want his snack. At least after they'd been up and down the sidewalk half a dozen times it was clean — not a twig or a leaf or a pebble in sight.

However, it didn't help that the other kids in the neighborhood kept riding by. They weren't teasing Jamie or anything. A lot of them waved and said "Hi!" and "Nice bike." But they *were* zipping along, riding with just one hand, or even (well, maybe those guys were showing off a little) with no hands at all, and there was Jamie, red-faced and poking along.

Finally, Mary Anne convinced Jamie to stop — by convincing him that she needed to rest. And she did.

She fixed iced tea for both of them (it was too late for Jamie's snack by then) and she and Jamie sat on the front stoop, with the bicycle propped carefully next to it.

The neighborhood kids kept whizzing by on their bikes. Jamie's face, watching them, was sad and mad all at the same time.

Mary Anne racked her brain, trying to think of something to say to make Jamie feel better. Finally, she remembered the campaign for class president.

"Listen, Jamie," she said. "Kristy's running for president of our class at school. Do you want to help her?"

"How?" he asked.

"We can think up campaign slogans. You know, good things about Kristy and why people should vote for her, like they do on commercials when they want you to remember to buy what they're advertising."

Jamie perked up a little at that. "Kristy for pres, she's the bes," he said right away. He is a smart kid. (Which may be why he's having so much trouble learning to ride his bicycle. He hasn't fallen yet — but he can *imagine* falling. And because he's smart, he can imagine it vividly and clearly.)

Laughing, Mary Anne said, "Wait a minute. I'll get pencils and paper and we'll write these down."

She and Jamie came up with some silly slogans, some funny ones, and some good ones, too: "Choose Kristy or else" (that was Jamie's). "You can't miss with Kristy" (Mary Anne). And a terrific one: "Kristy for president of the class — make some changes and make them last" (both of them together).

It was fun, and Jamie seemed to forget about his bicycle woes for awhile. But Mary Anne didn't. Even after Mrs. Newton came back (Lucy's doctor said she was just perfect, which we all knew, of course) and Mary Anne was heading home, she was trying to think of a way for Jamie to overcome his fear of falling off his bicycle.

It wasn't going to be easy.

CHAPTER 7

When the campaign for class president started, everything seemed to move into high gear. Suddenly the halls were full of posters. Lots of SMS students started wearing buttons and ribbons.

Stacey had had a really good idea. Instead of making only posters, we'd also made lots and lots of photocopies of our "Kristy for president" slogan with the big K+ symbol beneath it. Claudia also designed a flier showing only the symbol, and we photocopied that and plastered dozens and dozens of them everywhere around the school, like on fences by vacant lots and things. According to Stacey, that was *the* way people in New York advertise things, especially rock concerts.

Of course, before we K-plussed everything, we asked permission. At SMS we had rules (naturally) about where you could put campaign stuff, but out of school, you couldn't be sure. Some people said no to the fliers and some said yes, and some seemed sort of surprised that we asked at all and just shrugged. As every baby-sitter and little kid knows, a shrug is like a maybe — it means yes. We wound up with more yeses than nos, so it hadn't hurt to ask.

And we used recycled paper and wrote at the bottom: "recycled paper/please recycle." That was Dawn's idea.

Mary Anne suggested that we keep moving posters around, and putting up new ones (we made all the posters reversible, too) so the campaign would stay interesting, and kids wouldn't see the same posters over and over again. We took turns going to school early to do that, but I tried to go early every morning, since I was the candidate.

When I couldn't help in the mornings, I'd do the poster switch after school, which is what I was doing when I realized I was going to be late for a meeting.

The meeting was for the candidates. As I dashed downstairs I wondered what on earth we could possibily have left to discuss. The candidates had already attended several meetings. The door was closed when I got to the room, but the meeting hadn't started yet. Mallory had saved me a seat, and I slid into it in my best Krusher team style.

"Safe," I muttered.

Mal grinned. "You didn't miss anything," she whispered.

"Tell me about it," I whispered back.

Mr. Kingbridge, the vice-principal, went over the rules of the campaign again, and I tried to use the time (subtly, of course) to look over some class notes. I have very good concentration, so it took Mal's elbow against my ribs to tell me that Mr. Kingbridge was saying something new about the school elections.

"As you know," he was going on when I looked up, "we want the candidates and the students to have every chance to interact in a meaningful way prior to the elections. Therefore, I am pleased to announce that in addition to a Campaign Day next week before the election, when candidates will be setting up booths in the school cafeteria and spending two hours in the morning campaigning . . ."

Including shaking hands, I thought. But not kissing babies!

". . . in addition to that," Mr. Kingbridge repeated, "we are going to give the candidates the opportunity to debate and to make two speeches."

Several hands shot up then, but Pete's was first. He stood up. "Excuse me, but when you say opportunity, do you mean it is a requirement?"

"It is, yes, going to be part of the campaign experience," said Mr. Kingbridge.

I groaned. I wasn't the only one.

From somewhere in the chorus of groans behind me I heard the phrase "dress to wear" (Grace, I thought, who else?) and that jerk Alan intoning, "Friends, Romans, countrymen, lend me your ears, your eyes, your noses . . ."

Beside me, Mallory wasn't groaning, though. She was absolutely frozen, her eyes enormous behind her glasses.

"Mal?" I said.

She turned to look at me and blurted out, in a panic, "A *debate*? Me? I've never done that before. This is awful!"

"You can do it, Mal," I said. "Don't worry." However, I was worried. Not because I had never debated anyone before. (I hadn't.) I just didn't know how I was going to find the time to do it.

Mr. Kingbridge answered a few more questions and then dismissed us.

"Oh, Kristy. A debate!"

Poor Mal. I tried to say something that would comfort her.

"Just think of this as reasoning with a much larger, older group of baby-sitting charges," I suggested.

"Somehow," said Mal, "that doesn't help."

I gave a strangled cry and Mal jumped.

Of course, it was Alan the Pest. He'd knuckled me in the arm.

"You do that again, Alan, and you'll be sorry!" I glared at him, but it didn't do any good. He just turned around and walked backwards in front of us.

"You and I are going to debate, Kristy. What do you think?"

I thought if he kept walking backwards, he was going to bump into the pole behind him, but I didn't say anything.

Alan crashed into the pole and slid to the floor. But the way he did it made me suspect he knew all along it was there. Mal giggled as he threw his arms out and pretended to be injured.

"Good grief," I said, stepping over his writhing body.

"A debate is an exchange of dialogue, Kristy!" Alan propped himself up on his elbow to call after us. "Somehow, I don't think you want to exchange dialogue with me."

"Brilliant, Alan," I said crossly. "Talk about someone who needs a baby-sitter," I went on to Mal.

"Or a keeper," suggested Mal. "A handler, an Alan-tamer."

"Now there's a thought . . . See, Mal? You're a fast thinker. You come from a big family where you automatically have to speak up for yourself. You're a great baby-sitter . . ." Mal blushed and shoved her glasses back up on her nose. "So you'll be fine in a debate."

"Thanks, Kristy." Mal turned toward her locker. "I know you'll do a super job. See, you're already convincing me. Sort of."

"Good . . ."

"See you tomorrow."

" 'Bye," I said absently.

Things will fall into place, I told myself as I opened the locker door. I caught my science book before it fell out — just the book I was looking for — and smiled. They *will* fall into place, I repeated to myself. Just like my locker. I can't get *every*thing done.

Things did seem to fall into place over the next few days. I even found time to make a special campaign button for Jamie that said, "Kris for pres, 'cause she's the bes," with "by Jamie Newton" on the bottom of it, to take to him the next time I sat for him.

But then another meeting was announced one morning over the loudspeaker. It was for that same day, right after school. Great, I thought. I had a conference then with my English teacher, Mrs. Simon. How was I supposed to go to the meeting *and* the conference? It just proved why I was needed as class president. This lack of organization was typical of SMS!

I was still fuming as I dashed out of Mrs. Simon's conference that afternoon, after agreeing to rewrite a report. "I know you can do better, Kristy," she kept saying. "I've seen what you do when you work up to your full potential." I thanked her, because I'd hate to drop my grade in English, but I didn't see when I was going to have time to rewrite a report.

I was ten minutes late to the candidates' meeting. Grace looked over her shoulder as I came in, then whispered something to the person sitting next to her, and they both snickered.

Ignoring them, I slid into a seat in the back of the room and tried to look intelligent as Mr. Kingbridge glanced over at me. He kept talking, but he also handed a piece of paper to a person in the first row, and gestured to him to pass it back to me. So then everybody turned around and knew I was late. Mal, who was sitting at the end of a row, gave me a sympathetic look.

The handout was about Campaign Day. It also listed the campaign rules in writing. Mr. Kingbridge read them aloud, then said, "Any questions?" and looked at me.

Even if I'd had any I wouldn't have asked! I jammed the paper in my notebook and shot out of there as soon as we were dismissed.

I had to get to the library, and fast. Charlie was going to pick me up in an hour, and I wanted some time to work on my newest science assignment. I *had* to get that done. It was due the next day, and I was baby-sitting for the Kormans that night. Which was, I'd decided, going to be the perfect time to do some of my homework.

Was I ever wrong!

I was almost late getting to the Kormans'. (Have you ever noticed that? How when a day starts getting crazy and hectic, it just keeps getting crazier and more hectic? And if you're late, you keep running later . . . ?) Luckily, I wasn't *really* late. Which is good, because it is very important for members of the BSC to show how responsible they are, and being on time is a big part of being a responsible baby-sitter.

So I was a responsible baby-sitter — just in the nick of time. Skylar, who is a year and a half old, had already started crying because she knew, probably by the way her mother and father were rushing for the door, that they were Going Out and Leaving Her.

Melody, who is seven, was standing in the hall watching her parents in an abstracted sort of way, like they were people in a movie. Bill, Mrs. Korman told me, was upstairs doing his homework.

"We'll be back by ten," Mrs. Korman told me. "Everyone has had dinner, but Bill and Melody can have dessert in a little while — it's ice cream. You know where everything is, of course."

"Have a good time," I said.

" 'Bye," said Melody.

"Waaah," said Skylar from her playpen.

I picked Skylar up. "Waah, waah," I said softly. "Is that any way to say hello?"

"WAAAAAh," howled Skylar, struggling in my arms. I checked her diaper. No problem there.

"Maybe she's sleepy," suggested Melody. "You could read to her."

"Good idea, Melody." I shifted Skylar and headed up the stairs. "Why don't you pick out a book and we can read to Skylar until she gets sleepy."

Melody ran ahead of me into her room. "Skylar has books, but they don't have enough words," she told me.

By then Skylar's wails had become the long babbling sounds of unhappy protest that babies make. She was winding down. Good, I thought. A couple of pages and she'll be sleeping like a baby!

But Skylar is a real individualist. I took the book Melody gave me, *Bedtime for Frances*, and started reading. Skylar kept complaining. I read to the end, with Melody standing at my shoulder, looking at Skylar and at the book, and Skylar kept complaining.

"Another book?" asked Melody.

"Okay," I said. I wondered if I could read my history homework assignment to Skylar. That would probably put her to sleep.

We read *Goodnight Moon* and *Runaway Bunny*. Skylar's complaints were in the whimper range now, but they were definitely still there.

"Let me try," said Melody. So I handed the books over to her. She picked up *Goodnight Moon* and began to read in a singsong voice.

And it worked! As Melody turned the last page, Skylar sighed and burrowed into sleep.

"Good work, Melody," I whispered. We crept into the hall. Now I could start on my homework.

But Melody had other ideas. "I'll help you with the ice cream," she said.

"Ice cream?"

"Dessert," she reminded me.

"Okay," I answered. "You tell Bill and we'll

rendezvous in the kitchen. Let's coordinate our watches."

Melody looked puzzled and held up her bare wrist. "Aha," I said. "When the big freckle gets past the wrist bone, then you'll know it's time for ice cream."

"Silly," said Melody.

A few minutes later Bill followed Melody into the kitchen, saying, "There's no such thing as freckle ice cream."

"Freckle ice cream *time*," said Melody, holding up her wrist. "And I bet there is so freckle ice cream."

"Yes . . . vanilla. It has those little freckle flecks," I teased.

"See," said Melody.

"What about Macadamia Nut? *Big* freckle ice cream." Bill made a gagging noise.

"Or Rocky Road — freckle and marshmallow melting skin ice cream! Ooooh!" shrieked Melody.

"Or with raisins — freckle and *wart* ice cream," added Bill.

"Oooh, oooh, oooh!" Melody cried.

"Whoa, whoa, whoa," I said. "What we have is Chocolate Chip."

"Yuck," said Bill. "Ice cream with moles."

"Double yuck," said Melody.

I set the dishes in front of them. "Okay,

guys, they're just chocolate chips. Not moles."

"I don't want any moles in my ice cream," said Melody.

"Me either," said Bill.

Great. I'd created another monster. For the longest time, Melody and Bill had believed a monster lived in their toilet. Now they believed, or liked to believe they believed, that chocolate chip ice cream was full of moles.

I took a bite of my ice cream. "See? Just chocolate."

Melody stared at me. "Yuck, Kristy."

"Okay, then pick the chocolate chips out."

Melody bent her head over the bowl and carefully began picking out the chocolate chips with her spoon and lining them up on the table.

"They look like chocolate chips to me," I said.

"Moles," said Melody.

"Kristy, can you help me with my homework?" asked Bill.

I sighed. I needed help with *mine*. But I said, "Sure. After you finish your ice cream."

"Grrreat. Stupendous," said Bill. He started picking the chips out of his ice cream, too.

I looked down at my own ice cream, which was melting into a vanilla and chocolate chip puddle. I wasn't going to pick out the moles — er, chips. I was going to eat it all. Because I wasn't going to get to my homework that night. That was clear.

I took a big bite of the ice cream.

"Eeew," said Melody.

"Yumm," I said, smiling.

If I couldn't get to my homework, I wasn't going to worry about it. I'd think about it in the morning.

CHAPTER 8

Have you ever noticed how fast tomorrow always comes? Like when you have homework to do? (I did finish my homework after baby-sitting for the Kormans. I got up extra early that next morning, and *just* managed it.) Or when you have to be at school early?

We — the candidates — had to be at Stoneybrook Middle School half an hour early on Campaign Day to set up our booths. Claudia and Mary Anne also got up early. Then they came by to help me carry stuff into school (Charlie had agreed to drive us) and to give me some tips about dressing.

"Why can't I just wear jeans and a nice shirt?" I asked.

"A light blue shirt would be good," said Claudia. "I read somewhere that light blue looks best on television."

"This is not television, Claud. Just the SMS

cafeteria. But I *do* have a light blue sweat shirt."

"Kristy. No sweat shirt," said Claudia firmly.

"Why don't you wear your black pants?" asked Mary Anne. "They look good."

"Okay," I said, digging through the closet.

Claudia was doing some digging, too. "Here. Why don't you ever wear this?"

"This" was an enormous sweater of a sort of creamy brown, with little black and green stripes running across it. I shrugged.

"Try it on," said Claudia.

At last I emerged, black pants, sweater, loafers. "I still look preppie," I complained. But I really didn't look too bad.

"Kristy!" a voice called.

"That's Charlie — come on." We gathered the stuff together, staggered down the stairs, and headed for school.

The cafeteria rang with people talking, shouting, pushing tables, and jockeying for the best place.

"Here," said Mary Anne. "Not too close to the end."

"And not too close to Alan," put in Claudia.

We set up the booth, which Claudia had designed. My logo appeared on red posters, over and over again. We had buttons, ribbons, and a handout that told all about me and what

I wanted to do. Claudia had designed that, too. It looked like a report card. Beside each point was the column for the grades, and in every column it just said "K+." It looked pretty cool. It was concise, effective, and distinctive. And serious. I wanted to convey how serious I was.

Which some people didn't. Alan, for example, had dressed in balloons. He looked like a big bunch of grapes. Everyone who took a button and put it on got to pop one of the balloons.

You could tell right away he was going to be a big, noisy hit.

Mal, looking nervous, was sitting at her booth with Jessi. Behind her was a big drawing of a clock, and written across it was "Time to let Mal keep the minutes!"

"That's great, Mal," I said.

"Have a clock," said Jessi. She handed me a button designed like a clock with the slogan on it.

"This really is great," said Mary Anne. "Oh, Mal, you're sure to win. I wish we could all vote for you."

"You can, when Mal runs for student council president," said Jessi.

"No way," said Mal, and we all laughed.

"Uh-oh," said Mary Anne. "Speaking of

time, here comes everybody."

We headed back for my booth. Campaign Day had started at SMS.

The next two hours were a blur, but a very distinct blur. Alan, who'd chosen a spot near mine (so much for planning), came to visit me almost right away.

"Go on, Kristy," he said. "Stick a pin in me."

"Don't tempt me," I answered. "What are you trying to say, Alan?"

"It doesn't matter what you say, Kristy. It's whether people remember you. First principle of advertising."

"This is a campaign for class president, Alan. You're not trying to sell breakfast cereal or something."

Alan flapped his arms and made the balloons flutter. "Are we having a debate?"

"No!"

Just then someone said to me, ' What *is* your platform?"

At last! A real question. Someone who was interested in the issues. A voter who wanted to become an *informed* voter.

I picked up my report card. "If you'll look at this card, you'll see the issues I am addressing. For example, I think we need to do something about our assemblies. They could be a lot more interesting. We could poll the students and find out what type of people they might like to see at the assemblies — "

"Nobody's going to listen to students."

"They will if you show them you care. And you can show them you care by voting for me."

Just then someone popped several of Alan's balloons at once. Amid shrieks and laughter, people began to drift away.

"Wait a minute," I said.

"They'll be back," said Mary Anne. "There's a lot to see."

Claudia reappeared.

"Where have you been?"

"Grace," said Claudia glumly.

"What?" I cried.

"Go see."

"I'll be right back." I headed in the direction Claudia had pointed, and then wished I hadn't.

Gruesome Grace and Creepy Cokie were in a booth set up to look like a studio. Cokie had slung a video camera over her shoulder. A monitor was perched on the table. Beneath a huge, glittering banner that said, "Meet THE candidate for class president," sat Grace. Her makeup was about three feet thick, and she was wearing a pale blue sweater, matching stir-rup pants, and a ton of jewelry. Grace was sitting and talking to people from our class, one by one. While she talked, Cokie taped them, and the event was being shown live on the monitor.

Kids were standing three-deep around, trying to watch. And if that wasn't bad enough, Cokie was also taking their pictures with a Polaroid while they sat with Grace beneath her banner. They got to keep the pictures.

"I don't believe this," I said to myself. I also instantly thought of another idea for my campaign. From now on, there had to be a limit to how much money anyone campaigning for office could spend.

"This must have cost a fortune," muttered someone at my elbow.

"No kidding," I answered, turning before I realized who it was. "Pete!"

"Hi, Kristy."

"Hi," I said.

"Not the best place for a booth, is it?" He nodded toward his own booth, directly across from Cokie's.

"Mmm," I said. I was surprised, a little. Pete's booth was serious, too. He had fliers and had buttons that said "Pete for President" and "Vote for Pete, for SMS's sake!" Basic, but also serious.

"I have to get back," I said.

"Good luck," said Pete.

"Oh! Uh, good luck," I answered.

"I hope Alan runs out of balloons soon," said Mary Anne when I returned. When I didn't answer, she asked, "How bad is it?"

"Remember when Claudia was talking about television?" I asked. "And I said this wasn't television?"

Mary Anne nodded. Claudia smiled.

"It is television. Only it's Grace's TV show. She and Cokie have a video camera here."

"Wow. I can't believe her parents let her take their video camera."

"You know what?" said Claudia. "I bet it doesn't matter. I bet plenty of candidates have been elected without major media campaigns."

"Major media campaigns?"

"You know, we did a media blitz of our own. The whole school knows the K+ symbol."

"Media blitz?"

"And I have more ideas, too." Claudia picked up one of the buttons and examined it intently.

"You'll win," said Mary Anne. "We just have to work extra hard."

"Extra hard," I repeated. "You're right, Mary Anne." I picked up a poster and a button, and said to a crowd of students passing by, "Excuse me. I'd like to show you a *very* interesting report card . . ."

The bell finally rang and the candidates began to clean up. We had gathered almost everything together when a nastily familiar voice said, "How are you feeling about being the underdog in this campaign, Kristy Thomas?"

Grace and Cokie were standing behind me. Cokie had trained the videocam on me.

"How about, 'Underdog bites back'?" I suggested, stepping up close to the camera. "Are you getting that, Cokie?"

Cokie backed up a little but kept the camera rolling.

"You are so immature," said Grace.

I bit back the retort that it takes one to know one. Instead I shrugged. "You're entitled to your opinion, Grace. Or anybody else's, since I doubt you ever have any of your own."

"What do you mean?"

"It's a difficult concept, Grace. . . . Are you getting this, Cokie?"

"Turn it off, Cokie. Let's go." Grace glared at me. "The best man will win."

"Grace," I said. "The best woman — and the best candidate — is going to win. So why don't you just go somewhere and get some more practice at being a loser?"

I couldn't believe I said that. I heard Mary Anne gasp behind me, and knew she couldn't believe it, either. Good grief, this campaign *was* making me crazy.

I almost said I was sorry (apologizing to Grace — double good grief!), but she turned and flounced away, with Cokie behind her.

Bending over, I picked up a piece of purple balloon.

"A+, Kristy," I muttered to myself disgustedly.

I had planned on spending the rest of the day resting, sort of with my eyes open, at my desk. That plan got scorched in science when we were reminded of the major, major test coming up the next day.

And I had Krusher practice.

A short practice, a quick dinner, homework, and then cramming for the test?

I glanced at the science book and my notes. No.

Could I skip the homework? No.

I could try to skip dinner, but somehow, I didn't think that would go over so well with Mom and Watson.

That left the Krushers.

The first thing I did when I got home was call the Krushers and cancel practice. I hated doing it. And I hated telling everyone it was canceled.

"Practice is *important*," Jamie kept insisting when I told him, and I knew he was thinking about his bicycle, too.

"It is, Jamie. I know. We'll practice soon."

But I couldn't say how soon. I wasn't going to make any more promises that I couldn't keep.

CHAPTER 9

Tuesday

You guys told me about Jamie Newton's NEW BICYCLE. But I still didn't quite get it. Until I arrived at the Newtons' this afternoon and discovered that my baby-sitting job had turned into a bike-sitting job. Or maybe a bike-holding job...

"Have you seen my new bike?" That was Jamie Newton's first question.

Dawn was prepared. She laughed and said, "I haven't seen it, but I've heard about it. I've heard it's beautiful."

Jamie said, "It's exactly perfect."

Mrs. Newton had just left. It was a perfect afternoon. Lucy was lying on her back in her playpen on the porch, making pedaling motions with her legs and having an urgley-talk conversation with herself, with gurgles of laughter in between the urgley-words. Jamie was pulling on Dawn's hand, trying to steer her in the direction of his bicycle.

"First, why don't I make something like lemonade or iced tea, Jamie? We can let it chill while we're practicing, okay?"

Jamie didn't look too thrilled, but he followed Dawn into the kitchen. She found some lemons and sugar, and gave Jamie the job of squeezing the lemons (after she'd cut them).

He seemed to enjoy it for awhile, concentrating so ferociously that Dawn had to smile.

"That's a lemon-face, Jamie," she told him.

"What's a lemon-face?" Jamie kept his face scrunched up while he juiced another lemon.

"It's the face you make when you squeeze lemons. See?" Dawn picked up half of a lemon and demonstrated, making a scrunched-up face of her own. Jamie laughed and made an even worse face.

After that, he invented six more lemon faces to go with the six lemon halves left that needed squeezing, and Dawn made lemon faces back while she stirred the lemonade. When it was done, Jamie did a taste test.

"Is that a lemon-face I see? Again?" asked Dawn.

"Sour," replied Jamie.

Dawn tasted it.

"Lemon-face!" crowed Jamie. He handed Dawn the sugar, and she spooned a little more in, even though it was white sugar. (Dawn would have used brown sugar, or even honey.)

Tasting it again, Jamie made another face, a big goofy-grin face, watching Dawn carefully. She caught on. "A lemonade face?" she guessed.

Jamie shrieked with laughter, and Lucy, who now was sitting in her high chair, shrieked, too. Dawn put the lemonade in the fridge, picked up Lucy, and let Jamie lead her outside. She waited while he wheeled his bike out of the garage.

"It's a beau-, uh, a very cool, handsome, perfect bike, Jamie."

"I know," he answered solemnly. "Can we — may we — practice now?"

"Sure. Let me get Lucy settled first." Dawn took Lucy over to her playpen and put a bright purple cloth ball near her. Lucy turned her head sideways and stared at it, then began talking to it. Babies don't know that everything doesn't answer. (Or maybe grown-ups don't know that things do. . . .)

"Dawnnn!"

"Coming." She gave Lucy a quick pat and then went back to Jamie who was holding up his bike.

She stopped in surprise. "Jamie, where are your training wheels?"

"I told Daddy to take them off," he answered. "Training wheels are for babies."

"But — "

"Look." Sure enough, a group of older boys were swooping up and down the street.

"None of *them* have training wheels."

"And you're ready to try riding your bike without training wheels now, too?"

Jamie nodded emphatically. But his voice wasn't so emphatic when he added, "Yes. Now."

"Okay, what do we do?"

"Hold my bike while I get up."

That was easier said than done. Poor Jamie.

He put one foot on the pedal and Dawn, who didn't quite realize how off balance it would make the bicycle, staggered back.

Jamie hopped off, quick as anything. His eyes were huge. "You dropped me!"

"No. I just wasn't ready."

"You *can't* drop me." Jamie's voice grew shrill.

"I won't. I promise. It's just that — " Dawn stopped. She was going to say, "It's just that without the training wheels, your bike is really unsteady." But she didn't want to scare Jamie any worse.

"It's just that I wasn't ready. That's all."

"Okay." Jamie got back into position, put his foot on the pedal, and waited. Dawn held the bike firm. Satisfied, Jamie grabbed her shoulder with one hand (which almost threw her off balance again), and swung up onto the bike seat.

"I'm ready to go," he announced.

Dawn held onto the seat and the handlebars to keep the bike upright. But even doing that, it was an extremely unsettling trip to the end of the driveway. Jamie kept wrenching the handlebars, pulling Dawn sideways. She had to struggle to keep from falling over, bike, Jamie, and all.

It didn't take her long to realize, either, that Jamie wasn't pedaling hard enough to get any momentum going. She was not only holding him up, she was pushing him forward. And sure enough, when they reached the end of the driveway, Jamie insisted on getting down, "helping" Dawn turn his bike around, and getting back up again.

Meanwhile, it seemed that every kid in the neighborhood had decided to ride his bike down Jamie's street. Dawn saw Jamie glance at them from time to time with a sad expression. But most of the time he was wearing his bicycle variation of the lemon-face: eyes scrunched up, frowning, his lips pressed tightly together.

They headed up the driveway and back down again. Dawn's arms were getting tired, her legs were aching, and her back was beginning to hurt.

"Jamie," she began.

"Watch out!"

"Wh-what?" Dawn swung around, half expecting to see a car bearing down on them — and then spent the next minute teetering precariously. Jamie didn't help. He was wrenching the handlebars around and flailing his legs wildly. One of his feet kicked Dawn in the stomach.

"Uhh." It knocked the wind out of her, but it also knocked her backward a little, and she was able to straighten the bike out.

"Jamie! What is it? Are you all right?"

"Stop, stop, stop!"

Dawn looked around wildly, and then gradually, remembering what she had read in the BSC notebook, it — dawned — on her. She looked down.

Sure enough, there in the driveway was a branch from the maple tree, with a couple of leaves still attached to it.

"That branch?" she asked. But she knew the answer.

"We have to move it," declared Jamie.

This was twice as hard to do without the training wheels. But Dawn finally managed to kick the branch out of the way with the toe of her sneaker.

As they rode slowly up the driveway, Dawn heard Lucy's voice. She wasn't talking to the purple ball or to herself anymore. She sounded fretful.

"Jamie," Dawn began. But before she could suggest that he'd had enough practice for one afternoon, the front wheel wobbled, then turned completely sideways. Jamie, his bike, and Dawn all went down in a heap.

Dawn managed not to fall all the way, but she landed in a sort of tripod above the bike and Jamie. By the time she'd straightened up, Jamie had begun to cry.

Pulling the bike off Jamie, Dawn checked

him for broken bones and for bumps. Fortunately, he'd just skinned his hands and one elbow.

"Come on," she said. She helped Jamie to his feet, being careful not to touch his skinned places, and led him into the house. She got the first aid kit out of the bathroom cabinet, then brought it and Jamie to the porch where she could keep an eye on Lucy.

As carefully as she could, Dawn wiped off Jamie's cuts and scrapes and put some ointment and Band-Aids on them. By the time she'd finished, Jamie had stopped crying. But his face had gone from lemon to mule.

Frowning ferociously, he announced, "I'm never going to ride that stupid bicycle again."

"Jamie . . ." Just then Lucy began to cry in earnest. Dawn picked her up. She wasn't wet. Maybe, thought Dawn wryly as she gave her a little juice in a bottle, the purple ball had said something to her she didn't like.

She walked Lucy up and down, and Lucy gradually stopped crying. Her eyes closed.

"Jamie, I'm going to take Lucy to her crib. Stay on the porch. I'll be right back."

Jamie nodded, staring straight ahead and still scowling.

What am I going to tell him? Dawn worried the whole time she was putting Lucy down for her nap. In fact, she held an entire conversation with herself. She imagined saying to Jamie, The important thing is, after you fall, to get up and try again. But then her self said back, he needs those training wheels. He's not ready to ride without them. But how, she asked herself, can I convince him to put them back on? And how, another part of herself asked, can I manage to walk up and down that driveway, pulling that bike ONE more time?

Returning to the porch, Dawn took a deep breath. "Hey, listen," she started to say.

But Jamie wasn't listening to her at all. He was watching the other kids flash by on their bicycles, their wheels spinning with silver flashes in the late afternoon sun. He was listening to the sounds of wheels on the pavement and the gears clicking and the whir of the wind as they flew by.

Gently Dawn put her hand on his shoulder. Poor Jamie, she thought.

He turned.

"Dawn?" he said.

"Yes?"

"Dawn, can we practice on my bike some more?"

CHAPTER 10

I didn't believe it.

Quickly I flipped the test over, so no one could see it.

Not that anyone was trying to copy me or anything. No way. Not even if they'd wanted to.

Because I'd just *failed* the test. There was a big red 60 at the top. Which was not surprising when you saw how many red X's there were by my answers.

I don't know why I couldn't believe it, but I just couldn't. I mean, I don't get 60s. Generally, I'm a good student, even in subjects I'm not crazy about. Like science.

But I wasn't a good student anymore. Part of me had to admit that, looking at those big (enormous) red numbers. Part of me said I should have been able to guess the right answers, just this once. And part of me was mortified.

I thought of Claudia, too. She's not good at

school, and she doesn't get great grades. I wondered if she was actually used to seeing these kinds of numbers at the tops of her tests. Somehow I didn't think it was something anyone could get used to.

Except maybe Alan.

The bell rang and gratefully I shoved the awful test into my notebook, then shoved that deep into my pack. I told myself I didn't have time to think about it. I told myself to concentrate on what I was really good at. Just by stepping out of this room, I knew I'd see the signs: K+ — KRISTY FOR PRESIDENT.

Uh-oh. Would this mean I couldn't run? No. It was just one test. All I had to do was study and —

"Kristy?"

I jerked to a stop. It was Ms. Griswold. She smiled.

"You know, Kristy, everybody has bad days."

"I guess."

"I think you're having a bad one now."

I smiled a little. What an understatement. "That's a fact," I said.

She smiled, too. "A scientific fact. Another fact is that you are a good student, generally. I have to say, your grade surprised me."

"Me, too."

"Did you study?"

I shifted my weight. I wanted to lie and say that I had. But I hadn't. The test was telling the truth.

"No. I guess I . . . I guess I earned that grade."

The answer seemed to satisfy Ms. Griswold. She nodded slowly. Then she said, "Kristy, I know you are running for class president. I know you are the president of a thriving business. I don't usually do this, but under these circumstances, I want you to retake this test."

Who would ever think anyone could be so excited by the words "retake this test"?

Ms. Griswold pulled her lesson book toward her and turned the page. "How about tomorrow at lunch?"

I thought quickly. No BSC meeting this afternoon, and no baby-sitting job, either. How had I wound up with a whole free afternoon? Never mind. I'd have plenty of time to study. Maybe I could even ace the test.

"Great!" I said. "Thank you, Ms. Griswold."

"You're welcome. Don't be late to class, now."

"I won't. And thank you again!" I hurried out.

I kept on hurrying for the rest of the day. I spent lunch in the library, doing homework that was due that afternoon. I spent every spare minute between classes checking on posters. (Was it my imagination or had someone been knocking all of mine askew. Someone named, say, Grace?) Study hall was spent on more catching up.

This afternoon, I was definitely going to study science. Big time.

But I got home after school and met . . . David Michael, wearing his Krushers hat and T-shirt.

Krushers practice! I'd forgotten I'd rescheduled it.

"Are you ready, Kristy?"

"Uh, David Michael . . ."

"We need to practice. You said so."

"Yes. You are absolutely right. I was just going to say give me a minute to get suited up."

"Okay." David Michael sat down at the kitchen table and stared at the clock. He really *was* going to give me only a minute.

I couldn't help but smile. As I walked by him I gave the bill of his hat a little yank.

"Hey!" he said.

"Maybe a few minutes," I said, and raced to my room to change.

It was a perfect day for softball. Everyone else seemed to think so, too. Most of the Krushers were already waiting for us when we arrived at the field.

"Plaaaay ball," shouted Karen as we walked up.

"First we should practice some basics, okay?"

"Plaaay basics." Karen went into gales of laughter and about half the team went with her.

I waited a minute to give them a chance to giggle themselves out. After all, the Krushers are not your usual softball team. For example, the average age of a Krusher team member is 5.8. And one of the youngest players, Gabbie Perkins, is two and a half and doesn't quite understand the game yet. We throw Gabbie a wiffle ball and stand very close to her when it's her turn to bat.

But age doesn't mean everyone doesn't try hard, and isn't good at *something* — even though not all of them are home run hitters, or fielders with rifle throws to first.

The giggling lessened and I held up my hands.

Then I looked over at Matt Braddock, who is just about our best player and who is also deaf. He was laughing, too. A lot of the kids know some sign language now (especially when it comes to playing softball), so they can talk to Matt. Someone had told him the joke, too. And I realized also that his sister, Haley, who can use sign language at top speed, was there to translate, in case.

But holding up your hands is universal, I guess, for GET QUIET. (I mean, look at how many principals and teachers use it.) Anyway Matt got quiet, too, although he kept this huge grin on his face.

"We're going to practice fielding grounders, okay?"

"What's a grounder?" asked Karen.

"I know, I know," said Jackie Rodowsky. "It's a ball that is hit along the ground."

"Good, Jackie." Jackie looked extremely pleased. He's sort of a, well, a walking disaster. Wherever Jackie goes, look out! The sound of something crashing or breaking or being bumped into is not far behind. But he's probably one of our toughest players. He never gives up.

"Does everyone understand? Okay. Now, what you do is, you get your body behind the ball. You don't bend over with your legs apart, because then the ball would go right through them. And you put the tip of your glove all the way to the ground. That way the ball doesn't roll underneath it. But even if it did, your body would be there to stop it. Right?"

I looked at the circle of suddenly serious faces.

"Okay, Matt — why don't you just come

100

roll a ball to me and I'll demonstrate catching a grounder."

After we'd tried a few, I divided everyone up into twos and let them practice.

I stared off into the outfield.

It's funny how, when you have so much to do, and so much to think and worry about, your mind can just start thinking of nothing at all. I mean, it goes on a mini mind vacation, without warning.

At least that's what was happening to me. The big, puffy clouds drifted overhead, the sun shone, and I drifted along with them, basking mindlessly in — mindlessness.

I don't know how long I hovered there. But suddenly I realized that someone was standing next to me, staring.

I looked down. It was Karen. Her hands were on her hips. The one with the baseball glove on it made her look like she was growing a wing.

"Uh, yes?"

"Have we practiced enough?"

I glanced around. David Michael and Linny were sitting on the ground, rolling the ball to each other. Matt and Nicky Pike were using bats like golf clubs to hit the ball back and forth, pretending they were playing golf (or croquet, maybe). Jackie was wandering around in right field, looking for something.

(The ball?) The team wasn't practicing much of anything.

I gave myself a mental shake, raised the whistle, and blew. Everyone looked up instantly.

"Come on in," I called. They trotted eagerly to me. The poor Krushers. While I'd been watching the clouds, they'd been getting bored. It really wasn't the same, practicing when the coach wasn't paying attention and helping you out.

"Okay, let's play a game. And we'll concentrate on making really good catches. They don't have to be perfect. Just do your best and remember what I told you."

I divided the teams up and sent them out. Since they were uneven, I went out to right field (which is traditionally where you put your least experienced player. Not much happens in right field because most batters are righthanded and they hit to left field). I thumped my glove and shouted, "Play ball!"

Claire Pike, who is five and prone to tantrums, was up first. She swung and missed. She swung and missed again.

"Keep your eye on the ball," called Karen. (One thing about coaching Karen — she never forgets anything you tell her!)

Claire stared hard at Matt, who was pitching. She leaned over a little, squinting, watching the ball.

Matt threw a fast pitch. Claire swung — and hit it! The ball klunked down, rolled about a foot, and died.

She stood looking at it.

"Run!" screamed Karen.

Claire wrinkled up her brow. Then she started toward first base. She kept looking back at the ball.

Good grief! Was she still keeping her eye on the ball?

"Don't look *now!* RUN!" I shouted.

Both Matt and the catcher dove for the ball. It disappeared between them, and Claire stopped watching it. She ran as hard as she could to first base.

Safe!

"Good work, Claire," I said.

She frowned suspiciously. "You're on the other team," she said, and turned her back on me.

I couldn't help but laugh.

It felt good to laugh. It seemed as if I hadn't laughed for a long, long time. Not much to laugh about right now, I reflected. The big fat red 60 on my science test loomed before my eyes. I *had* to study tonight. I *had* to . . .

"Kristy!" shrieked David Michael.

I came to earth abruptly. Jackie Rodowsky, the Walking Disaster, was running at top speed toward first base. Claire, still stealing anxious glances at the ball, was on her way to second. And the ball was streaking across the grass toward me.

Everything happened at once. One minute I was staring at the ball openmouthed, trying to gather my wits. The next minute, in a kind of super slow motion, I was stretching my glove down toward it.

Too late. The ball took a sharp, wicked hop and smacked me hard in the shin.

"OWWW!" I grabbed my leg, hopped once, lost my balance, and fell over.

"Get the ball," someone shouted. There was a mad scramble around me, then Matt held the ball up.

"Time out," called Karen.

I sat up, holding my throbbing shin, just as Claire touched home plate.

"I made it!" she cried.

"No, you didn't." Karen trotted past her, on her way out to right field.

"I did too!"

"It was already time out," said Karen. "Kristy fell down."

Claire's face scrunched up. She took a deep breath, turned bright red, and began to throw a tantrum. "Nofe-air! Nofe-air!"

We're all pretty used to Claire's tantrums by now, so, keeping my eye on her, I stood up and tested my leg.

I looked at the circle of anxious faces. "It's all right. Okay, listen up. This was a *key* lesson. Pay attention!"

"You stopped the ball," said David Michael diplomatically.

"Yeah," several people murmured.

I looked at their faces. They'd started to smile. The Krushers were a great team, no doubt about it.

"Um, let's play ball," I said. "But I'm going to coach from the sidelines."

I walked gingerly back toward the third base line with Claire, who had stopped tantruming.

"Does it hurt?" she asked.

"Only when I laugh . . . Okay, Claire, you go back to third, okay?"

Her face started to scrunch up again, and I added quickly, "That way, you get to run home again."

She thought about it for a moment, let her breath out, and trotted back along the baseline.

I leaned over, pulled my cap down, put one hand on each knee, and called, "Play ball!"

For the rest of the practice, I made myself pay attention.

Making yourself pay attention is exhausting.

After practice that afternoon, I felt pretty tired. And by the time dinner was over and I'd disappeared upstairs to study for my science test, I was wiped out. But I had to do it. Ms. Griswold was giving me a second chance not to fail.

I opened my notebook, picked up my highlighter . . . and the phone rang.

"Kristy?" It was Claudia.

"Hey, Claud. Listen, I've got to study, I — "

"Yeah. Don't you hate it? Unless it's art, but that's not work. That's art."

"I'm not any good in art," I said. "Or science, either, at least not right now."

"You're a good student, Kristy. And science is very organized. At least that's what my teacher always says. So you should be good at science because you're so organized."

I sighed. "I wish it worked that way."

Claudia went on, "So, have you written your speech yet?"

"Speech?" I gasped. I looked over at my calendar. Sure enough, there it was. Tomorrow the class assemblies were going to be held for the first round of speeches.

"Oh, no!" I cried.

"You haven't?" asked Claudia.

"I'm about to. Right now. Listen, Claudia, you saved my life. I gotta go."

"Good luck," said Claudia.

"Good-bye," I said.

When I sat down at my desk again, I pushed the science book out of my line of vision. Tomorrow morning. I'd get up early tomorrow morning and study. And between classes. And maybe during the assembly.

But first I had to write a speech. A really, really good speech. I closed my eyes, imagined myself at the podium.

Ladies and gentlemen? No. Fellow students? No.

I pulled my notebook toward me, turned to a blank sheet, and began to write.

CHAPTER 11

"Thank you," I said to the mirror. I was practicing my speech.

Someone tapped on the door to my room.

"Kristy?" It was my mom.

"Come in," I said.

She stuck her head around the door. "It's late."

"I know. I'm almost done."

"Anything I can help with?"

For a moment I was tempted. But what could she do? I could tell her how overwhelmed I felt, but that wouldn't make the feeling go away. I took a deep breath and shook my head. "Thanks, but I'm just in a crunch right now."

"Well . . ."

"So much work, so little time," I explained.

My mother smiled. "Don't forget to sleep," she said.

"I won't. 'Night."

"Good night, Kristy."

After she'd closed the door, I turned back to the speech. It was an okay speech. It *sounded* okay. At least I thought it did. I looked at the clock. Too late to call Mary Anne and read it to her. Her father was a lot more lenient these days, but I don't think *anybody's* parents would appreciate a phone call at this hour.

It *could* be a better speech. Maybe tomorrow, if I had time . . . no, I'd forgotten about the science test. I looked over at my bed, then back at the pages of the speech, then at the science book. I got up and put the science book under my pillow and climbed into bed. I didn't *really* believe the knowledge would seep into my brain during the night, but I was desperate.

My eyes closed as soon as I turned out the light. I thought I'd worry so much I wouldn't be able to sleep. But sleep was no problem . . . then.

The problem came at about two A.M. I opened my eyes and stared into the darkness. Boom. One minute I'd been sound asleep (although not dreaming about science or science books) and the next minute I was wide awake.

And my mind was going a mile a minute. Speech. Baby-sitters Club meeting. Baby-sitting jobs — maybe I could let some of those slide for now. The Krushers (my shin gave a sympathetic throb). All the duties of being president of my class. At least I had experience being a president; being president of the BSC had taught me just how many responsibilities a person in charge has.

Maybe I should temporarily resign from the BSC. Or go on inactive status. Would that work? The thought gave me a sharp pain in the stomach, but I reminded myself it would only be temporary.

Of course, with every thought, I had to turn over, or thump the pillow, or pull on the covers. It wasn't like being in bed at all. It was like swimming in choppy water, just trying to stay afloat.

I looked at the clock. Good grief. Almost an hour had passed. I *had* to get some sleep, or I'd be one of the walking dead the next day. Instead of Kristy Plus, my slogan would be Kristy, Rest in Peace.

Closing my eyes, I willed myself to stop thinking.

It worked for about a minute. Then I found myself staring into the dark, my mind going around and around, thinking the same things over and over again.

Finally I got up, very quietly, pulled my science book out, and took it to my desk. I turned on the lamp. I opened the book. If anything would put me to sleep, it would be studying science.

It was weird, studying in the middle of the night. I mean, I'd heard my brothers complain about pulling all-nighters, but this was the closest I'd ever come. Turning the pages of the book seemed to make a lot of noise. And the house was so quiet. Staring at the pages, listening to the silence, I decided that big houses have a different kind of quiet than smaller houses, like the one we used to live in. Smaller houses were a noisier quiet. They creaked. Sounds didn't have so far to travel, maybe.

Maybe there was a scientific explanation . . . Science. I jerked my thoughts back to the book. I studied. I kept waiting to get sleepy.

But it was a long time before I did.

One thing about not getting enough sleep: You don't have enough energy to worry.

The next day for the first round of speeches, assemblies were held by grade in the auditorium. The candidates had to sit in the front row. Just my luck, I got the seat next to Alan. He crossed his eyes. I ignored him.

Behind me, I could feel the whole eighth grade breathing down my neck. Don't be silly, I told myself.

Grace leaned across Alan toward me. "Is that your speech?"

I looked down at the paper-clipped pages in my hand.

"Yes. Why?" (That shows how out of it I was. I *knew* better than to ask Grace anything.)

"No reason," said Grace. She leaned back and made a big point of opening a leather folder. Tucked inside was a thin stack of 3 x 5 cards, with typewritten words on them. Grace looked up and caught my eye. Satisfied, she smiled and closed the folder again.

Typical Grace, I thought. But typed 3 x 5 cards do not a good speech make.

Alan didn't seem to have any speech notes at all. I couldn't see Pete from where I was sitting. He was on the other side of Grace.

Our principal walked up to the podium and cleared his throat and waited. I glanced back. Mary Anne, a few seats behind me, caught my eye and nodded, holding up her thumb.

Where was everybody else? Before I could scope out the assembly anymore, the rustling and shuffling and whispering died away. Our principal smiled.

"We are here today for the preliminary round of speeches by our candidates for the offices of eighth-grade president, vice-president, secretary, and treasurer. Each candidate will have three minutes to present his

112

or her platform. At the end of the speeches, if we have time, they will field questions. We'll begin with the candidates for secretary."

Good. I slid my science notes out under my speech notes and began to read over them. Somehow, all that reading in the middle of the night hadn't helped. The facts just wouldn't stick in my brain.

"Grace Blume," said Mr. Taylor. Grace stood up, smoothed her hair, and walked calmly to the podium. She looked very pulled together up there, smiling at the assembly.

"When you choose your class president, you want to choose someone who can truly represent you," said Grace.

She paused. She put one of the little white cards behind the other, then read the next one.

"I will be the leader you need." (Pause, change cards.) "We work hard." (Pause, change cards.) I'm going to leave out the rest of the pauses, but you get the idea.

Grace went on. "But you wouldn't have to work quite *so* hard if you had the right leader.

"As your leader, I would see to it that we didn't have to work so hard. We need to enjoy ourselves once in awhile. For example, our football team has been winning! Isn't it time we celebrated that? And what about dances?"

And so on. I rolled my eyes, not caring if Grace saw me. I knew she was shallow, but this was ridiculous. She was making all kinds of impossible promises. But people applauded when she was done, as if they didn't know the difference.

Finally it was my turn. It was a long walk to the podium. I stood for a minute looking out at everyone. And everywhere I looked, I saw a member of the BSC — Dawn in one corner, Mary Anne near the middle of the room, Logan a little further back, Claudia in another corner, Stacey in the front. For a moment I was disconcerted: We usually sat together.

Then as I glanced around the room again, meeting their smiles wherever I looked, I realized they'd split up on purpose.

Suddenly, I didn't feel so dim and sleepy. I smiled at the whole assembly.

"I'm not up here to make a lot of promises that I — or anyone — can't keep," I began. Grace's eyes narrowed. "What I am here for is to talk about responsibilities. We're expected to study, to participate in school activities, to go to classes, to follow certain rules. We do that pretty well, I think. So it seems to me that we should have more responsibility. I don't mean more rules to follow. But more of a chance to prove ourselves. For example, we have a class play every year. Who gets to choose which play we put on? We have no

114

input into that decision. I think it is time we did. I think we should have a committee of people from our class to choose which play we perform . . ."

As I outlined my ideas about school lunches and the Special Ed classes, I saw people nodding. They were listening! They agreed with me. And I was sure the applause as I sat down was louder for me than it had been for Grace (she, of course wasn't applauding at all). Anyway, I heard Claudia whistle (I think it was Claudia).

Then Alan got up.

The worst.

He stepped behind the podium and said, "Okay, everybody stand up."

There was a pause, then a buzz of talk.

"Come on," said Alan. "Up!"

The buzz of talk grew louder, but everyone eventually got to their feet.

"Good," said Alan. "Now, sit down again."

"What is this," said someone, "Simon Says?"

Alan waited, his arms extended, until the snickering, grumbling students sat down. Then he folded his arms across his chest.

"I've just proved to you what a good leader I am. You all did what I told you. So now I'm telling you to vote for me."

That was it! He left the podium and returned

to his seat, raising his clasped hands over his head at the rest of the class talking and laughing behind him.

I couldn't believe it.

After Alan, Pete seemed unbelievably mature. I grimaced. Alan was such a pest. Just his existence had made Pete look good. Although it hadn't hurt any of the rest of us, either.

"Every one of the candidates for class president has presented some good ideas," Pete began. "And when I'm president, I'll be glad to try to put some of those ideas into practice. I, too, believe that we should be part of the decision about what class play we perform each year. I'd also like to see greater editorial freedom extended to our school newspaper . . ."

I groaned. Boring.

"Assemblies could be better here at SMS, too. I'd like to be a part of a committee to take suggestions for speakers — speakers *we* would be interested in — and to help get those speakers.

"At least some of those assemblies should be pep rallies. We have a great football team — "

Pete paused while people broke into cheers. (I didn't cheer. I thought it was extremely manipulative to encourage the audience to cheer by talking about the football team.)

"But we have some other great athletes, too. They also deserve pep rallies."

I had to admit, it was an interesting idea. But was it practical? Wouldn't that mean we'd be holding pep rallies practically every ten minutes, if we included every team in the school? Like the fencing team? It would take some organizing . . .

"And that's only the beginning. But I need your help first — your help when you vote. Vote for Pete Black for president."

The applause was loud.

Okay ideas. Some of them.

I pulled out my science notes. I needed to use every minute to study for the make-up test at lunch. And I did. I had to hurry to get there on time.

Ms. Griswold was waiting for me.

"Sorry I'm late," I said.

She looked surprised. "You're not late, Kristy. Slow down."

"Oh. Well, anyway, I'm ready for the test."

Ms. Griswold smiled. "Good."

I slid into my seat, pulled out a pencil, and took the test from her.

"Good luck, Kristy."

Luck wasn't enough. Some of the material I'd studied came back to me — or was it just familiar from being on the test the last time?

Maybe I should have pulled an all-nighter. I went over and over and over the questions, and the answers, but I didn't feel good when I handed the test back to Ms. Griswold.

She took out her red pencil. It really got a workout. Finally, just before the bell rang signaling the end of lunch, she finished.

She looked up. "I'm sorry, Kristy," was all she said.

Numbly, I stood up and took the test from her hand. I felt my face turn red. I'd flunked. In fact I'd made an even lower grade.

"Thank you, Ms. Griswold," I mumbled and walked out quickly, before she could say anything else, ask any questions. What would I tell her anyway? I, Kristy Thomas, world-class organized person, was turning into a klutz and a failure? And it seemed that the harder I tried, the worse I did. I felt tears sting the backs of my eyes, but I pushed them away.

Stop it, I told myself fiercely. You're just tired. It's no big deal. It's just one test.

But I never, ever, in my whole life would have thought I'd fail the same test not once, but twice.

CHAPTER 12

Thrusday

Good greif. Jamie is a bicicle
monster! Really! Big time. If only
he hadnt taken those trainning
wheels off! But something good did
happen. Jaymi was trying to do to
much, to soon, and he finally saw
that. Maybe he (and we) can finally
start tamming the bicycle monster...

"*This* is a great outfit, Lucy," cooed Claudia, following Jamie outside. They were going to see Jamie's bike (what else?). Lucy, looking even more adorable than usual (if that's possible), was wearing lavender overalls with pink stars on them, a pink shirt, pink socks, and little purple sneakers with shoelaces that had stars and moons on them.

Jamie was wearing jeans, a long-sleeved T-shirt, sneakers, and a look of ferocious determination.

"Okay," he said, wheeling his bike out of the garage.

"Great bike, Jamie. See the bicycle, Lucy? Someday, you'll be riding a bicycle just like your big brother."

"No!" said Jamie. "Not for a long time."

Uh-oh, thought Claudia. Sore subject. Aloud she said, "Of course not. Not for years. It takes a lot of hard work, Lucy, and don't you forget it!"

Lucy said something in urgley, grabbed Claudia's hair (which was in a fat braid with seven bows in different colors tied up and down it) and pulled. It didn't hurt, because Lucy is a baby. But it definitely said, "I'm here. Pay attention to *me*."

"Lucy, you are too much," said Claudia,

carefully extracting the braid from Lucy's fingers.

"I want to practice riding my bike," said Jamie.

"Okay. Why don't I put Lucy in her stroller, and you can get on your bike and we — "

"No. You have to help."

Claudia's pretty easygoing, but she almost got annoyed at Jamie's bossy tone. Then she remembered the trouble he'd been having with the bike and softened. "Okay, Jamie. I'll tell you what, Lucy, it's the playpen for you for a little while, okay?"

So Lucy returned to her playpen on the porch to watch Jamie practice riding his bike. Fortunately, Lucy isn't one of those babies who is picky about what she watches. Watching Jamie and Claud go up and down the driveway seemed just fine with her.

Claudia knew what to expect from reading the BSC notebook. So she scouted out the driveway and made sure every single leaf, pebble, and twig were gone. Then she stood on one side of the bicycle and held it while Jamie climbed up on the other side.

"You know, Jamie, Kristy told me how she put the training wheels on . . ."

"They're gone now," Jamie replied.

They started down the driveway. Claudia

wasn't sure, but she thought Jamie was probably as shaky as ever. Even though they didn't run into any twigs or leaves, every time she let go the least little bit, Jamie wobbled like crazy.

And he fell more than once, in spite of Claudia's help. The front wheel would go one way, Jamie would make a dive, and all three of them (Jamie, Claudia, and the bike) would lose their balance. At least Jamie didn't cry. Claudia decided that he'd probably gotten a fair amount of practice at falling and was getting used to it.

But the third time he fell, Claudia thought she heard wailing. Only it wasn't Jamie. It was Lucy.

"Hold on a minute, Jamie," said Claudia, extracting herself from the tangle of bike and boy and heading for the playpen. Lucy's face was red and crumpled. Somehow, she'd managed to push her teething ring out between the bars of the playpen.

Picking it up and putting it back inside, Claudia leaned over and tickled Lucy's stomach. Lucy grabbed the ring and stuffed it in her mouth.

"Umm, good," teased Claudia gently. The red, scrunched-up look left Lucy's face and she waved her feet.

"Claudia!" said Jamie.

"Jamie, Lucy needs to play, too."

"I'm not playing," answered Jamie.

"I know," said Claudia. "You're working hard. But why don't we take a break?"

Suddenly Jamie wailed, sounding not much older than Lucy. "I can't. I can't!" He bent over and began to wrestle the bicycle upright.

What could Claudia do? She helped Jamie get back in the saddle, and they began to poke and wobble their way down the driveway.

Just then, one of the posse of bicycle-riding kids on the street, whom Jamie had been watching with such envy, wheeled to a stop at the curb. The others pulled up alongside him.

Jamie became stiffer and more red-faced. It didn't help. And all those kids standing there staring didn't make Claudia feel any calmer, either.

But they turned out to be just what Jamie needed.

As Jamie reached the end of the driveway, the first boy said, "You should slow down a little. What happened to your training wheels?"

"Took them off," said Jamie.

"Why? You hardly got to use them . . ."

"Because," said Jamie.

"You know what? It's easier if you use them for awhile first. You're trying to do too much. It's impossible."

Claudia held her breath, half expecting Jamie to jump in and start arguing, but he looked at the boy and said, "Really?" His tone of voice was so relieved, Claudia wanted to hug him.

Instead she asked, "Where *are* your training wheels, Jamie?"

"In the garage," he replied.

"I'll tell you what," the boy said, "if you put them back on, I'll help you practice."

"You will?" Jamie slid off his bike and took the handlebars from Claudia. She stepped back.

"Sure. Rich helped *me* learn to ride." The boy jerked his head toward one of the other boys, who nodded. "I practiced with two training wheels, then with one. Didn't I?"

Rich nodded.

"Really?" asked Jamie again.

The boy grinned. "Yeah. One wheel at a time. That's all you can do anyway, you know. One thing at a time."

"Can we practice tomorrow? I'll ask my mom and dad tonight to put the training wheels back on."

"Okay." The boy hopped on his bike and pushed off. "See you tomorrow, Jamie."

"Okay," Jamie called.

And just like that, the red-faced, stubborn, miserable bike monster was gone. Smiling sunnily, Jamie wheeled the bike around (with a little help from Claudia) and headed back up the driveway.

"I'm going to learn to ride my bike," he told Claudia. "They're going to help."

"That's great, Jamie."

Jamie wheeled his bike into the garage and smiled up at Claudia. "Want to take Lucy for a walk?" he asked.

"You think you have time for that now?"

"Oh, sure," said Jamie. "You can't practice all the time, you know."

Hiding a smile, Claudia said solemnly, "I know."

CHAPTER 13

"Kristy? Kristy!"

I jumped about a mile. "Karen!"

"I scared you, didn't I?"

"You did," I agreed. "I think you made me grow some gray hair."

"Let me see." Karen marched over to the sofa I was sitting on and stared. "Nope."

"Too bad."

"Why does hair turn gray? Why doesn't it turn some other color? Like green?" Karen wondered.

"I don't know."

"Mine's going to turn green *and* purple. I'll be a scientist and make it do that."

That reminded me of the science test. And the list I was making. Claudia's afternoon with Jamie kept coming back to me. *One wheel at a time.* You can only do one thing at a time. That was the trouble. I was trying to do about ten

126

things at a time. And not doing any of them well.

"Can you?" asked Karen.

"What?"

"Come decorate the pancakes. We're having a Sunday pancake lunch, and Nannie and Emily Michelle and David Michael and I are cutting up fruit and all this good stuff and we're going to make the pancakes into shapes and put faces on them."

"Can I just come have some pancakes later?"

"Oh, no! That's not as much fun, Kristy."

I sighed. "I know. I just have so much to do. I have to finish this list."

Karen looked at me mournfully. With her glasses, she is very good at it. But I truly had to get organized. I looked mournfully back at her and shook my head.

"Silly billy," said Karen. "Good-bye."

"Good-bye," I replied, and sighed again. Then I heard myself. Two sighs in two minutes. Not good. I am not a person who sighs much.

But I was making a list. I was going to become the most organized person on earth. And as soon as that happened, I wouldn't be so, well, disorganized. Things would get done. Things would be fine.

But the best-laid plans of mice and men —

and baby-sitters — go wrong. I knew my new organizational strategy was already in trouble by Monday afternoon, as I dashed up the stairs at Claudia's house, late for our meeting.

Claudia was on the phone, lining up a job. Mary Anne had opened the appointment book in her lap. Mallory and Dawn were throwing popcorn in the air, trying to catch it in their mouths. Stacey was leaning gracefully against the headboard of Claudia's bed, watching. Jessi was opening a bag of yogurt raisins.

My chair was empty.

"Sorry," I cried, rushing in. "I finished at the Papadakises' and then I tried to start my homework and the next thing I knew, Charlie was calling me and I was late." I collapsed in my chair.

Everyone stared.

"Okay, okay," I said. I straightened up and took a deep breath.

Mary Anne, who sees a lot, asked quietly, "What's wrong, Kristy?"

"I'm fine," I said. I looked around at my friends' faces as Claudia hung up the phone. "Well, maybe not fine, exactly."

"Exactly what?" said Dawn.

"Ms. Griswold called Mom and Watson about my science grade."

"Oh, no. The worst. Are you grounded?" asked Claudia knowingly.

"No. But they're going to 'monitor' my assignments — that's what they told Ms. Griswold — to make sure I complete my homework."

The phone rang and Claudia picked it up. I said quickly, "No jobs for me for awhile. Unless it's absolutely necessary."

"Oh, Kristy! Did they say you couldn't babysit?" cried Mallory.

I shook my head. "No, I did. But it's only temporary. I've just decided to cut back a little."

After the details of the baby-sitting job had been worked out and Claudia had called the client back, Mary Anne said, "What about your campaign? Are you ready for the debate yet?"

"Well, I'm almost done with my homework," I answered evasively.

"Kristy! That debate is important!" exclaimed Stacey. "You have to get ready for it."

"I *will*." Uh-oh! Did I sound as cranky as I thought I did just then? "Sorry, Stacey," I said quickly. "You're right. I'll get to work on it as soon as I get home. After all, I know what my position is. That's pretty clear-cut and simple. And Grace and Alan, lord knows, don't have a position. And Pete's not much better.

"Pete's okay," said Mary Anne.

"I didn't say he wasn't okay, Mary Anne.

But his platform, his *reasons* for wanting to be president are not much better than Grace's or Alan's . . ."

"Whatever Alan's reasons are," muttered Claudia.

Mary Anne looked stubborn, but she didn't say anything.

"Are you ready, Mallory?" I asked. Mallory's face turned red.

"I guess," she said.

"Your opening speech was good," Jessi announced firmly.

Mallory threw Jessi a grateful look. "I had planned to do a little more work on it tonight, though."

"You know, what you should do is relax," Jessi told her. "I read about this relaxation technique for stress. You lie down, and you picture yourself doing whatever it is — like giving the speech — just perfectly, once, from beginning to end. Then you go do something nice for yourself."

"Like eat ice cream with chocolate sprinkles and butterscotch topping," put in Claudia.

Mallory laughed.

"Hold the ice cream. I'll get to work on the debate tonight," I promised. "Now, if the meeting has already come to order, what about dues?"

"Right," said Stacey. "Thanks for reminding me, Kristy."

"What are presidents for?" I asked sweetly.

Everyone groaned.

That night, while Mallory was (maybe) practicing relaxation, I was doing my homework in world-record time. By nine-thirty, I was finished. Whew!

I pulled out a new notebook and opened it. I picked up my pen.

I remembered one of the rules of giving a speech: Tell them what you're going to tell them, tell them, then tell them what you've told them.

Hmmm. Useful, maybe, but this was a debate. I had to be absolutely clear on what I thought the goals of our class should be. And I had to be absolutely clear on what I thought were the weaknesses of the other candidates' goals. My goals had to sound like the best. Not hard, I reasoned, since they *absolutely* were.

"#1," I wrote.

The phone rang.

"We," I wrote.

"Kristy, it's for you," my mother called.

When I picked up the receiver a voice said, "Hello, stranger."

"Bart!" *Stranger?* Oh, lord. Was I going to

have to add Bart to my list of things to worry about?

I was starting to worry about the list!

"Well, at least you recognized my voice," said Bart.

"Lucky guess," I teased.

Bart laughed and I laughed, too. And I almost felt guilty about being on the phone, laughing! But I was glad he called.

Twenty minutes went by in no time at all. Then I told Bart, reluctantly, that I had to get off. "I have to get ready for the debate, you know."

"I wish I could be there," said Bart.

"Me, too," I replied, and we said good night.

I went back to my debate notes. "#1. We need to . . ." resolutely ignoring the ringing of the phone.

"Kristy." My mother's voice. "It's Jessi."

"Hello," I said, snatching up the receiver. "Listen, I'll have to talk to you tomorrow. I'm behind in my work."

"Geez, Kristy. What if you win the election? If you don't have time to talk to me, how will you have time to be president of the whole class?"

Jessi's words hit home. "Oh." I sighed again. "You're right, Jessi. But what can I do? I can't drop out of the race."

"Maybe you should drop out of something else, then," said Jessi.

"Like the human race," I muttered. I felt awful.

"What?"

"Nothing. Listen, Jessi, I really am swamped."

"I know. I'll talk to you tomorrow."

She hung up pretty quickly. I sat and stared at my paper.

"#1. We need . . . a president who has time to be a president. . . ." And it was time to find the time.

CHAPTER 14

The "Kristy for president" team had done a great job. Everywhere you went in SMS, the signs jumped out at you. The buttons were a huge success, too. I saw them all over the place: on backpacks and purse straps, hooked onto lockers and taped to notebooks. "Good visual coverage," declared Stacey. We would vote the Friday after the debate. The campaign was becoming intense.

It seemed as if people were more involved, too. Which meant, I thought, that the issues were important to us. We *did* care about our school, and we *did* want some responsibilities (besides homework and going to class). Furthermore, I thought that with this kind of support just for the campaign, we were showing everyone we were serious and willing to work and handle other responsibilities.

Responsibilities.

Suppose Grace won? I doubted she was

even capable of organizing a school dance. And I don't think she'd begun to think about all the work involved. Once she found out, that would be the end of Grace's participation. But what would we do? Impeach her? That would make a nice headline for the school newspaper.

Which reminded me of Pete and his campaign. He had one, or *maybe* two good ideas, but they were really only the sorts of things that would appeal to a minority of kids. Special interest groups. That was the phrase. Pete's campaign appealed to special interest groups.

Alan. Please.

It was my responsibility to run for president. Besides, so many people had worked so hard. (Including me.)

But not hard enough.

I thought about this over and over again. And I kept scrambling, squeezing in homework, a Krushers practice, a minimum of baby-sitting jobs.

You wouldn't think I would have a lot of time to think, but somehow I did. I was even catching up on my work a little bit. Part of the reason was I had simply put aside the campaign and my debate speech.

If Jamie had become a sort of bicycle monster for a little while, hadn't I become a sort of political monster?

I'd let down the Krushers, canceling practice and then not being there mentally when we did have one. I'd gotten the worst grade I'd ever made in science — twice. I'd been late to meetings — BSC meetings, campaign meetings — and close to late for baby-sitting jobs. I'd had to give up baby-sitting jobs (and money!). I'd hardly seen Bart. And I'd practically bitten Jessi's head off for telling me the truth.

Plus, now my mother and Watson had to monitor my homework as if I were a little kid.

All of those things were responsibilities, too. They were *my* responsibilities. And I wasn't living up to them.

It happened one night. I was sure I'd go straight to sleep, I was so tired. But instead, I lay in bed with my eyes open, thinking everything over one more time. Making my lists (again) of what I had to do (like homework, especially science), and what I wanted to do (like spend time with my friends and coach the Krushers and eat pancakes with faces on them).

But this time, when I finished my lists, I knew what I was going to do. The only way to do everything I wanted to do, and needed to do, and do it right, was not to run for class president. I was going to have to drop out of the race.

I said it aloud, for practice. "I have to drop out of the race."

It didn't sound so bad. It could have been worse.

I said it one more time. No. Not so bad at all.

Immediately I was sleepy, so sleepy that I didn't even know I'd fallen asleep until I woke up the next morning, ready to go, ready to do everything — except be class president.

I wasn't sure quite how I was going to go about telling everyone what I had decided. Silly ideas — like going around to all the posters and writing K— — came to mind. Or going to the principal's office and making an announcement over the PA system (except, of course, no one would have understood it). Probably, I could have just told the rest of the BSC and they could have spread the word for me.

Although I cringed to think how my friends would feel about my dropping out of the race. After all that work. I almost talked to Mary Anne about it. I knew she'd be calm and sensible and supportive (at least, I was almost absolutely certain she would be supportive). But then I thought of another way of handling it.

Once I made that decision, it was easy to quit worrying about that along with everything else. It must have shown, too, because that very next morning, Mary Anne (she's calm, sensible, supportive, *and* perceptive) said, as we walked into SMS together, "You must have finished preparing for the debate."

"I'm ready," I assured her. "Why?"

"You *look* ready. More pulled together." I looked down. I was wearing jeans and a crew-neck sweater, one of my standard uniforms.

"Kristy! I'm not talking about what you're wearing!"

"I know, I know."

We caught up to Stacey and Claudia then. They both looked great (I'd been so busy, I hadn't even *seen* anyone, it seemed like, even though I'd been seeing everyone almost every day. If that makes any sense.) Stacey had pulled her hair back into a braid with a silver hat pin stuck through it. She was wearing purple capri pants, soft black flat ankle boots, black-and-white-striped socks, and a black-and-white-checked shirt, only the checks were all different sizes. She had square silver earrings in her ears.

Claud's hair was down, but she was wearing a hat. On the green hat ribbon was pinned a "Kristy +" button. Her tights were orange and her dress was tie-dyed every color you could think of. She was wearing her feather earrings, and she'd drawn a star on her face next to her right eye.

"It's *great* to see you all," I said.

Everyone looked a little surprised. "Sure, Kristy," said Stacey.

"She's ready for the debate," Mary Anne explained, laughing.

"Ohhh. Good job, Kristy. Need any special art effects?"

I shook my head. "Thanks, Claudia, but I'm all set. "Now I only have to worry about science."

Claudia made a face.

"Don't worry," said Mary Anne loyally.

"Yeah . . . be happy," added Stacey.

Thinking about the science homework, complete and all correct (at least I was pretty sure it was) I laughed. "I am," I said. "I am!"

The day of the assembly, I joined the other eighth-grade candidates in the front row of the auditorium. After the principal explained the rules for the debate, he handed the podium over to the candidates so we could each make a one-minute opening statement.

This time, Grace didn't lean over to make snide remarks about my notes. She couldn't have, anyway, because I didn't have any. But she was busy shuffling through hers, looking worried. Alan was carrying a notebook stuffed full of papers, and a pen. Pete surprised me, though. He was holding one piece of paper, with typing on it. He looked like he knew what he was doing, and was pretty sure of himself.

"Now, Kristy Thomas, candidate for eighth-grade class president," said the principal.

I took a deep breath, stood up, and walked slowly to the podium. I gripped the sides of it (I was a little nervous) and looked out at everybody.

My friends were sitting together this time, in the middle of the auditorium: Mary Anne, Dawn, Stacey, Claudia, and Logan. Mary Anne gave me a big smile.

I smiled back at her and at everybody.

"I'm Kristy Thomas, and I'm *not* a candidate for class president."

A buzz swept through the auditorium, so I did what the principal did. I kept quiet and waited. While I waited, I looked at my friends.

I don't know what I expected, but they didn't look upset. Mary Anne was nodding slowly, thoughtfully. Claudia looked surprised, and she and Stacey (who also looked surprised) were whispering to each other. Dawn looked as calm as ever. And Logan was frowning a little.

The buzzing died down, so I went on. "I've enjoyed running for office," I said. "I've learned a lot. One of the most important things

I've learned is that a person shouldn't try to do too much. The office of president of the class is one with a lot of responsibility — especially if the new president wants to make changes. I think we need some changes, but I'm not the one to make them. I already have a lot of responsibilites. I want to do well at the things I am doing right now, and I want to have time to enjoy what I do. If I stayed in the race and won, I wouldn't be able to do the job right.

"I wish the candidates for president the best of luck. I know whoever is elected will do a terrific job. I'm sorry to withdraw from the race, but I think — I know — I am doing the right thing.

"I want to thank all of you for your support, and especially my friends." I looked down at the members of the BSC. They all seemed pretty calm now. Did they understand?

"Thank you," I said.

It was Mary Anne, I think, who started to applaud. Some of the other kids joined in. So the walk from the podium back to my seat wasn't so bad after all.

I'd done it! And it felt — okay. Even the smirk Grace gave me didn't change my mind. I listened to the rest of the debate in a daze.

When the assembly was over, Mary Anne was the first to reach me.

"Kristy!" she said, and hugged me.

The others were smiling. "Does this mean you're back in the baby-sitting business?" asked Dawn.

"Definitely," I said.

Claud held up her hand and I slapped it. "I'm still going to wear this button," said Claudia.

"A collector's item now," Stacey told her solemnly.

I grinned. Then my friends and I walked out of the auditorium together.

CHAPTER 15

I took down the last of Mallory's posters and put it on the pile.

"Whew," I said to Mary Anne.

"You can say that again. It's much easier putting *up* campaign posters."

"Yeah." We headed for Mallory's locker. She and Jessi had stacked a heap of posters beside it.

"What are you going to do with all the posters?" asked Mary Anne.

Mallory pushed her glasses up on her nose. "Turn them over and use them next year."

"And next year, I bet you'll be the incumbent," said Jessi.

"I don't know." Mallory looked doubtful. "Besides, even if I do get elected to secretary of the sixth grade, I don't know if that'll count for anything in seventh grade."

"Next year, run for president," I told Mallory as Claudia, Stacey, and Dawn appeared with armfuls of posters. "I can recommend a group of campaigners experienced in supporting presidential hopefuls."

"Good grief, Kristy," teased Stacey. "You're starting to talk like a politician."

"Or a newscaster!" Claudia let her posters slide to the floor. "It's almost time for homeroom and the big vote. Are you nervous, Mal?"

"Yes."

"Ah — an honest politician," teased Dawn.

"I'm a little nervous about the eighth-grade presidential race," I confessed.

"You did the right thing," said Mallory. "You don't have to worry now."

But Mary Anne understood right away.

"It would be unfortunate if the best person didn't win," she said.

"You mean it would be the *pits* if Grace Blume did," put in Claudia. "And she might."

"She's definitely spent the most money on her campaign," said Stacey. "For Grace, it's a big popularity contest. Too bad."

"Especially if she wins . . . but then again, what if Alan wins?"

"No way, Kristy."

"Pete could win," said Mary Anne.

The homeroom bell rang.

"Time to vote for Mallory," said Jessi. "Come on, Mal."

"Good luck, Mallory," said Stacey, and the rest of us chimed in with "good lucks" of our own. Then we headed for our homerooms to vote.

I voted for Pete. I wondered who else did. Mary Anne did for sure.

The day was nerve-racking, I'll admit it, even if I wasn't a candidate anymore. But Mallory *had* to win. And I'd decided who had to win as eighth-grade class president, too.

Finally, during last period, the PA system crackled to life.

And for once, it worked — sort of. Or maybe it just sounded clearer because everybody became absolutely quiet in order to listen.

The principal began with the sixth grade, starting with treasurer. Secretary was next: I held my breath . . .

"And" (crackle static) "sixth-grade secretary . . . Mallory Pike."

I let out a whoop. "All right, Mallory!" I didn't even care when everyone turned around to stare.

Then we had to listen to a lot more snap, crackle, static as the winners of the rest of the sixth grade and the seventh grade were read aloud. "Faster, faster," I muttered, but it didn't help.

Finally: "And the new pres-(screeech) the

145

eighth grade is . . . Pete Black!"

What a relief. I didn't let out a whoop, but I was suddenly *very* glad Pete had run for class president.

School was over after that, and for the last few minutes, while everyone else was talking, I thought about Pete's campaign. I wasn't crazy about his platform. But he'd made some good points (especially the ones that were similar to mine!). And he was serious about the job. Plus, he *had* said he'd liked some of the other candidates' ideas. Maybe I would catch up with Pete later and congratulate him and go over my ideas in detail . . . just in case he wanted to use them.

Yes. The best person had definitely won.

I was on time for our meeting that afternoon. But I wasn't the first to arrive. Everyone except Mallory had arrived ahead of me.

"Hey," I said. "What's the deal?"

Everyone stood up and applauded.

"You did good, Kristy," said Mary Anne. "We're proud of you. And . . . welcome back to being merely incredibly busy — instead of out of your mind."

"Thank you," I said. Just then, Mallory stepped through the door.

We stood up and applauded again, while Mallory turned pink.

"Speech, speech!" cried Jessi.

"No way!" said Mallory, grinning.

Then the phone rang. I sat in my chair and called the meeting to order, and Claudia began to hand around tropical-flavored jellybeans, Fig Newtons, and Frookie cookies (they're sweetened with fruit juice so Stacey can sometimes eat them, and Dawn does, too).

It was good to be back to normal. Toward the end of the meeting, I said, "You know what? Remember Pete said he thought the students should be the ones to choose the class play?"

"Um-hm," said Claudia around a mouthful of jellybeans.

"So?" asked Stacey.

"Well, listen. Suppose we get to do *Our Town*? And suppose I could try out and land the role of Emily? Wouldn't that be *fantastic?*"

A moment of silence greeted me. Then Mary Anne groaned, Mallory and Jessi started to laugh, and everyone else joined in.

I realized what I'd done.

"Well," I said. "If it's not softball season, I might . . ."

"Kristy!" said everybody together.

"Meeting's over," said Stacey, when she stopped laughing. "Come on."

"Where?" asked Mallory.

"To celebrate your victory, Mallory! Surprise! We planned everything. Charlie's going to drive us downtown. We're going to pig out." Claudia wadded up the empty jellybean bag, buried it in her wastebasket, and jumped to her feet.

"Wait a minute," I said, "let me see if I can fit this into my schedule . . ."

"Kristy," said Mary Anne. "Come *on!*"

Laughing, we all trooped out to celebrate Mallory's victory.

Dear Reader,

In *Kristy for President*, Kristy finds herself involved in too many activities, and realizes she needs to drop some. Just like Kristy, I tend to be very busy. Because I'm so busy, I find that the best way to manage my time is by scheduling, scheduling, scheduling. (Mary Anne would be so impressed!) Tuesday, Wednesday, and Thursday are "typical" work days. They're reserved for writing manuscripts and outlines, for reading galleys (books before they're published), and for answering mail. Friday is devoted to other kinds of work. I'm the president of two foundations, the Ann M. Martin Foundation and the Lisa Novak Community Libraries. On Fridays, my assistant and I visit organizations that have received grants from the foundation, or we sort donated books into small children's libraries which we give to shelters, day care centers, and other places where books are needed. I'm also on the boards of three additional organizations — I have to squeeze that work in whenever I can. You may be wondering what I do on Mondays. Mondays are reserved for sewing — my favorite activity. I think it's important to make time for yourself, as well as for work.

Happy reading,

Ann M. Martin

L. GODWIN

Ann M. Martin

About the Author

ANN MATTHEWS MARTIN was born on August 12, 1955. She grew up in Princeton, NJ, with her parents and her younger sister, Jane.

Although Ann used to be a teacher and then an editor of children's books, she's now a full-time writer. She gets the ideas for her books from many different places. Some are based on personal experiences. Others are based on childhood memories and feelings. Many are written about contemporary problems or events.

All of Ann's characters, even the members of the Baby-sitters Club, are made up. (So is Stoneybrook.) But many of her characters are based on real people. Sometimes Ann names her characters after people she knows, other times she chooses names she likes.

In addition to the Baby-sitters Club books, Ann Martin has written many other books for children. Her favorite is *Ten Kids, No Pets* because she loves big families and she loves animals. Her favorite Baby-sitters Club book is *Kristy's Big Day*. (By the way, Kristy is her favorite baby-sitter!)

Ann M. Martin now lives in New York with her cats, Gussie and Woody. Her hobbies are reading, sewing, and needlework — especially making clothes for children.

Notebook Pages

This Baby-sitters Club book belongs to _____ .

I am _____ years old and in the _____

grade.

The name of my school is _____ .

I got this BSC book from _____ .

I started reading it on _____ and

finished reading it on _____ .

The place where I read most of this book is _____ .

My favorite part was when _____ .

If I could change anything in the story, it might be the part when

_____ .

My favorite character in the Baby-sitters Club is _____ .

The BSC member I am most like is _____

because _____ .

If I could write a Baby-sitters Club book it would be about ___

_____ .

#53 Kristy for President

In *Kristy for President*, Kristy runs for president of the eighth grade while Mallory runs for secretary of the sixth grade. If I could run for any class office, I would run for _____ because _____ _____. Kristy's campaign slogan is "K + ." My campaign slogan would be _____ _____. I would want _____ to be my campaign manager, and _____ _____ to be my campaign workers (like the other BSC members are for Kristy). If elected, some of the changes I would make in my school are _____ _____ _____. If I were voting for the president of my grade, I would vote for _____ _____ because _____ _____ .

KRISTY'S

Playing softball with some of my favorite sitting charges.

A gab-fest

Me, age 3. Already on the go.

My family keeps growing!

with Mary Anne!

David Michael, me, and
Louie — the best dog ever.

81 *Kristy and Mr. Mom*
Kristy's stepfather Watson has a new job!

89 *Kristy and the Dirty Diapers*
Will Kristy lose the Krushers when they change their name to the Diapers?

95 *Kristy + Bart = ?*
Are Kristy and Bart more than just friends?

#100 *Kristy's Worst Idea*
Is this the end of the BSC?

Mysteries:

4 *Kristy and the Missing Child*
Kristy organizes a search party to help the police find a missing child.

9 *Kristy and the Haunted Mansion*
Kristy and the Krashers are spending the night in a spooky old house!

15 *Kristy and the Vampires*
A vampire movie is being shot in Stoneybrook. Can Kristy and the BSC find out who's out to get the star?

19 *Kristy and the Missing Fortune*
It could all be Kristy's — if she and the BSC crack the case.

25 *Kristy and the Middle School Vandal*
Cary Retlin is up to his old tricks — and Kristy has to stop him!

Portrait Collection:

Kristy's Book
The official autobiography of Kristin Amanda Thomas.

Collect 'em all!

100 (and more)
Reasons to Stay Friends Forever!

More titles... ➤

❏ MG48226-2	#82	Jessi and the Troublemaker	$3.99
❏ MG48235-1	#83	Stacey vs. the BSC	$3.50
❏ MG48228-9	#84	Dawn and the School Spirit War	$3.50
❏ MG48236-X	#85	Claudi Kishi, Live from WSTO	$3.50
❏ MG48227-0	#86	Mary Anne and Camp BSC	$3.50
❏ MG48237-8	#87	Stacey and the Bad Girls	$3.50
❏ MG22872-2	#88	Farewell, Dawn	$3.50
❏ MG22873-0	#89	Kristy and the Dirty Diapers	$3.50
❏ MG22874-9	#90	Welcome to the BSC, Abby	$3.99
❏ MG22875-1	#91	Claudia and the First Thanksgiving	$3.50
❏ MG22876-5	#92	Mallory's Christmas Wish	$3.50
❏ MG22877-3	#93	Mary Anne and the Memory Garden	$3.99
❏ MG22878-1	#94	Stacey McGill, Super Sitter	$3.99
❏ MG22879-X	#95	Kristy + Bart = ?	$3.99
❏ MG22880-3	#96	Abby's Lucky Thirteen	$3.99
❏ MG22881-1	#97	Claudia and the World's Cutest Baby	$3.99
❏ MG22882-X	#98	Dawn and Too Many Sitters	$3.99
❏ MG69205-4	#99	Stacey's Broken Heart	$3.99
❏ MG69206-2	#100	Kristy's Worst Idea	$3.99
❏ MG69207-0	#101	Claudia Kishi, Middle School Dropout	$3.99
❏ MG69208-9	#102	Mary Anne and the Little Princess	$3.99
❏ MG69209-7	#103	Happy Holidays, Jessi	$3.99
❏ MG45575-3		Logan's Story Special Edition Readers' Request	$3.25
❏ MG47118-X		Logan Bruno, Boy Baby-sitter	
		Special Edition Readers' Request	$3.50
❏ MG47756-0		Shannon's Story Special Edition	$3.50
❏ MG47686-6		The Baby-sitters Club Guide to Baby-sitting	$3.25
❏ MG47314-X		The Baby-sitters Club Trivia and Puzzle Fun Book	$2.50
❏ MG48400-1		BSC Portrait Collection: Claudia's Book	$3.50
❏ MG22864-1		BSC Portrait Collection: Dawn's Book	$3.50
❏ MG69181-3		BSC Portrait Collection: Kristy's Book	$3.99
❏ MG22865-X		BSC Portrait Collection: Mary Anne's Book	$3.99
❏ MG48399-4		BSC Portrait Collection: Stacey's Book	$3.50
❏ MG92713-2		The Complete Guide to The Baby-sitters Club	$4.95
❏ MG47151-1		The Baby-sitters Club Chain Letter	$14.95
❏ MG48295-5		The Baby-sitters Club Secret Santa	$14.95
❏ MG45074-3		The Baby-sitters Club Notebook	$2.50
❏ MG44783-1		The Baby-sitters Club Postcard Book	$4.95

Available wherever you buy books...or use this order form.

Scholastic Inc., P.O. Box 7502, 2931 E. McCarty Street, Jefferson City, MO 65102

Please send me the books I have checked above. I am enclosing $_____
(please add $2.00 to cover shipping and handling). Send check or money order—
no cash or C.O.D.s please.

Name_____ Birthdate_____

Address _____

City_____ State/Zip _____

BSC5962

THE BABY-SITTERS CLUB®

by Ann M. Martin

Collect and read these exciting BSC Super Specials, Mysteries, and Super Mysteries along with your favorite Baby-sitters Club books!

The Baby-sitters Club books continued...

☐ BAI47049-3	#11 Claudia and the Mystery at the Museum	$3.50
☐ BAI47050-7	#12 Dawn and the Surfer Ghost	$3.50
☐ BAI47051-5	#13 Mary Anne and the Library Mystery	$3.50
☐ BAI47052-3	#14 Stacey and the Mystery at the Mall	$3.50
☐ BAI47053-1	#15 Kristy and the Vampires	$3.50
☐ BAI47054-X	#16 Claudia and the Clue in the Photograph	$3.99
☐ BAI48232-7	#17 Dawn and the Halloween Mystery	$3.50
☐ BAI48233-5	#18 Stacey and the Mystery at the Empty House	$3.50
☐ BAI48234-3	#19 Kristy and the Missing Fortune	$3.50
☐ BAI48309-9	#20 Mary Anne and the Zoo Mystery	$3.50
☐ BAI48310-2	#21 Claudia and the Recipe for Danger	$3.50
☐ BAI22866-8	#22 Stacey and the Haunted Masquerade	$3.50
☐ BAI22867-6	#23 Abby and the Secret Society	$3.99
☐ BAI22868-4	#24 Mary Anne and the Silent Witness	$3.99
☐ BAI22869-2	#25 Kristy and the Middle School Vandal	$3.99
☐ BAI22870-6	#26 Dawn Schafer, Undercover Baby-sitter	$3.99

BSC Super Mysteries

☐ BAI48311-0	The Baby-sitters' Haunted House Super Mystery #1	$3.99
☐ BAI22871-4	Baby-sitters Beware Super Mystery #2	$3.99
☐ BAI69180-5	Baby-sitters' Fright Night Super Mystery #3	$4.50

Available wherever you buy books...or use this order form.

Scholastic Inc., P.O. Box 7502, 2931 East McCarty Street, Jefferson City, MO 65102-7502

Please send me the books I have checked above. I am enclosing $ _____
(please add $2.00 to cover shipping and handling). Send check or money order
— no cash or C.O.D.s please.

Name_____Birthdate_____

Address _____

City_____State/Zip_____

Please allow four to six weeks for delivery. Offer good in the U.S. only. Sorry, mail orders are not
available to residents of Canada. Prices subject to change.

BSCM496